Flip the Script

ALSO BY LYLA LEE

I'll Be the One

Flip the Script

LYLA LEE

KATHERINE TEGEN BOOKS
An Imprint of HarperCollins Publishers

Katherine Tegen Books is an imprint of HarperCollins Publishers.

Flip the Script
Copyright © 2022 by Lyla Lee
All rights reserved. Printed in the United States of America.
No part of this book may be used or reproduced in any manner whatsoever without
written permission except in the case of brief quotations embodied in critical articles
and reviews. For information address HarperCollins Children's Books, a division of
HarperCollins Publishers, 195 Broadway, New York, NY 10007.
www.epicreads.com

ISBN 978-0-06-293693-6

Typography by Molly Fehr
22 23 24 25 26   PC/LSCH   10 9 8 7 6 5 4 3 2 1

First Edition

To anyone pursuing an "impossible" dream,
whether that be career-wise or in love

Chapter 1

I REACH OUT AND CARESS THE FACE OF THE BOY I'm supposed to love.

"I love you," I say.

"I love you, too," he replies, his voice all quiet and tender. "I've had feelings for you for a long time."

On TV, Bryan Yoon is usually so goofy and cute, but now, when he's absolutely serious, his gentle eyes have a magnetic pull to them that's hard to resist. This kind of star power is probably the reason why millions of girls all over the world have posters of Bryan and the other members of NOVA, one of the top K-pop boy bands in the world right now. And why even ahjummas like my mom and her friends are members of their fan café.

I know why I'm supposed to have feelings for him, but in the end, what *really* gets my heart racing is the thought of Korean fried chicken.

Yummy and crispy and fried to a golden brown, I think while staring into my costar's eyes. *Just the right amount of greasy, perfect with some pickled white radish and a can of Diet Coke.*

Don't get me wrong, Bryan is really cute. But do I like him as much as I love my favorite food in the entire universe? No. Will I ever like him as much? Probably not. I've actually never felt that intense kind of emotion for *any* human being—but I imagine this is what true love is like. And I must have been convincing, too, because from his chair behind the camera, Director Cha shouts, "Cut! That was fantastic. That's a wrap for today."

As soon as the director's turned away, Bryan's doting smile becomes a lopsided smirk.

"That was pretty good, newbie," he says, running his hand through his swept-back hair. "Been practicing?"

One of his assistants hands him a *box* of water, and he chugs it while waiting for my reply.

"I still don't get why you insist on calling me newbie," I say. "I've been in this industry for four years, while this is your first year as an actor."

He shrugs. "Yeah, but I've been in the entertainment industry *in general* for much longer than you . . . *and* this is your first year breaking out big, isn't it?"

"Fair," I concede. Sometimes I forget that even though his professional name is English, Bryan comes from an entirely different world than me. While I only moved to Korea a few years ago, he spent all his life here in Seoul, training with prep academies and music companies since he was in elementary school.

Bryan reaches out and ruffles my hair like I'm a little kid and he isn't just one year older than me. "Just don't lose your nerve after the premiere tonight. Good luck, Hana!"

I push him away and he laughs, giving me a peace sign on the way to his manager's van. Usually I'd reply with something snarky, but today I don't even have the mental capacity to do so. I'm far too anxious about tonight.

Most Korean dramas, unlike American TV shows, follow a live-shoot system. Even though today's the premiere, we've only shot the first four episodes so far, and we'll continue to shoot the rest of the show as new episodes air every week on Fridays and Saturdays. Live shooting can be overwhelming and stressful since it keeps production schedules tight enough to film and edit each of the remaining episodes within a week or two. But it's also cool since we can adjust things based on viewers' reactions and make last minute changes, if needed. For better or worse, tonight we'll know exactly what audiences all over the world think of our show. And I'll learn what millions of people think of my acting.

The biggest challenge will be finding the right balance between keeping true to my character and adjusting my performance according to feedback. I heard a lot of actors in movies or American TV shows never read reviews or watch themselves on the screen. But when people are reacting to a show as we're making it, it's hard to ignore their responses. And it's probably not a good idea to overlook them, either.

On the bus ride home, I search for news articles released today about our show.

Breaking News: Highly Anticipated Fantasy K-Drama *Fated Destiny* Set to Premiere Today at 9 p.m. KST!

Bryan Yoon Dishes on His New Show *Fated Destiny* on the Eve of Its Premiere

Why *Fated Destiny* Starring Bryan Yoon Is THE Biggest K-Drama of 2022

From the way the press is writing about it, you'd think *Fated Destiny* was a one-man show. But I'm glad it's at least on everyone's radar. Even now on the bus, I overhear conversations about our show.

"I'm so excited to watch Bryan's new series!" says a middle schooler who's sitting a few seats behind me. "I'm for sure going to watch it after I'm done with cram school."

"I'm just going to watch it on my phone. The tutors don't care about what we do as long as we finish our work anyway."

"*Really?* Mine are super mean and take our phones away."

"Oh, huh. I always assumed they don't care, but maybe I'm

just too sneaky for them to notice!"

They laugh, and I'm still smiling to myself when the first girl says, "Wait, speaking of *Fated Destiny*, did you see the girl Bryan's costarring with? What's her name again, Jang Hana? Jin Mina? How did a complete nobody like her land that role?"

I bite my lip to stop myself from correcting her. *It's Jin Hana!*

The other girl shrugs. "I think I recognize her from *Superstar League*. Didn't she play the foreign exchange student from America? She was pretty good."

"She *better be* to star with *our* Bryan."

"To be honest, I hope she sucks. Celebrities end up dating their costars all the time. We can't lose Bryan to someone like her!"

Resisting an urge to sigh, I navigate to one of my playlists on Spotify, which is a collection of kick-ass girl power anthems from my favorite K-pop singers. I tap on a song by Skye Shin, who just debuted this year but is already topping the charts. Skye's Korean American like me, so I relate to a lot of her songs.

As I listen to her strong, confident voice, I feel my shoulders loosening up.

I'm not naive enough to think that people will be watching the show for me. I *know* that most of the world will watch our K-drama out of morbid curiosity, since it's the show that's supposedly so good that Bryan turned his back on music at the peak of his music career for. But I'm determined not to get outshined by him. Not when I have so much riding on this show.

Just as I get off at my bus stop, I get a call from Sophia, my manager.

"How are you holding up?" she asks me in English.

After a whole day of speaking Korean, hearing English is admittedly comforting. I may look like I was born and raised here in Korea, but I'm from Florida. I grew up splashing around in the warm turquoise waters of the Atlantic Ocean, not looking across the Han River like I am now.

Since I've always spoken Korean with my parents, I'm fluent, but I'm still more at ease with English. Meanwhile, Sophia was born in Korea but hopped back and forth between here and the US throughout her life, so she's perfectly good at both Korean and English in a way I can only aspire to be.

"I'm fine," I say. "Okay, that's a lie. I'm terrified, but I'm trying to chill. I just overheard a bunch of middle schoolers trash-talking me."

"Nerves are understandable. But try to enjoy tonight as much as you can. You earned this big debut. And remember, good or bad, buzz is buzz. Tonight's premiere is going to be huge!"

I let out a quick sigh. "You're right. As always. Hopefully no one makes fun of my Korean."

"They're not going to. You practiced so much! And honestly,

your Korean wasn't even that bad in the first place. Why are you worrying about it now?"

While I lived in a not-so-diverse part of the American South, I spent countless nights cuddled up on the couch with my mom watching every Korean drama I could get my hands on. K-dramas were my way of feeling like I belonged *somewhere* when I lived in a place where no one but my parents looked like me.

But when I was scouted by an entertainment company in middle school and actually moved to Seoul four years ago, it didn't take long for me to realize I'm only as Korean as a sweet potato stuffed crust pizza. Yeah, sure, sweet potato stuffed crust pizzas are a staple of *Korean* Pizza Huts. But they're still pizzas. Which means they're not very Korean at all.

I may not feel Korean enough, but tonight everything depends on convincing people I belong here. My parents gave up the life they had in the States to move back across the world with me. And everyone involved with the show worked so hard to get us to this point. As the co-lead, my performance affects the ratings and consequently their jobs.

Tonight everyone will be watching.

"Hana?" Sophia says, bringing me out of my thoughts.

I sigh again. "Sorry, I'll try to relax."

"Excellent idea. Eat yummy food, put on a facial mask, anything that'll help you feel better. Talk to you after the premiere?"

"Yup. Thanks, Sophia."

By the time we hang up, I've arrived at home. It's 8:45 p.m., fifteen minutes before the show's premiere.

The moment I open the door, Mom and Dad hug me. Mom's holding a bag of Flamin' Hot Cheetos, my favorite snack, while Dad's got a pair of chopsticks in one hand.

I almost burst into happy tears then and there. As much as I love eating Cheetos, I hate getting the red dust on my fingers. So I eat them with chopsticks. My parents know me so well.

"We're so excited to watch the show!" says Mom.

Not much for words, Dad doesn't say anything. But he doesn't have to. His proud smile says enough. He's a strong and silent Asian patriarch type, so a smile from him is the equivalent of glowing praise from someone else.

My parents work long hours, so I know how hard it must have been for them to make time for this. My stomach aches from how thankful I am. My life isn't perfect, but one thing I definitely lucked out on are my parents.

I plop down into my usual space on the couch, right in between Mom and Dad. We rarely have time to watch TV together anymore, but when we do, I cherish every second of it.

Too nervous to stay still, I bounce my leg up and down as I snack on my Flamin' Hot Cheetos, plucking each one out of the bag with my chopsticks and popping it into my mouth.

Mom, like she always does, notices immediately and says in a firm but gentle voice, "Hana, you know bouncing your leg like that is bad luck! You're shaking your good fortune away."

I grew up with my parents telling me not to do seemingly random things like shaking my leg or leaving the fan on before I sleep at night. Back in Florida, I thought it was just my parents who had these oddly specific superstitions. But when we moved here, I heard ahjummas at a seolleongtang restaurant gossiping about fan death and realized those beliefs are part of what made my parents Korean in ways that I'm not.

I half pay attention to the commercials before the premiere, alternating between looking at my phone and the TV. When I first moved to Korea, the ads fascinated me since they're all visually stunning. But they also disturbed me a little bit since everyone looks unnaturally bright and happy, like they live in some alternative utopian society. And everything is so "perfect," too, with grandparents sitting at tables with two parents and two children—a boy and a girl, of course.

Sure, my own family is pretty heteronormative and nuclear, but that doesn't mean I for sure want a family like that in the future. I'm bi, and I don't know who I'll end up with yet. And I'm nowhere close to even thinking about kids. I wish Korean media had more flexibility for other lifestyles.

When the last ad fades into black at exactly nine p.m., I sit up straight, with one hand in Mom's and the other in Dad's.

"It's going to be great," Mom says. "Appa and I are so proud of you."

Dad squeezes my hand, and I squeeze his back. His hands

are a little sweatier than normal, but I smile and hold on tight.

Four months and counting of rehearsals and shooting days. Endless days and nights of filming. All the blood, sweat, and tears that the other members of the cast and crew, my parents, and I have put into this show so far. Everything has come down to this.

I let out one last slow breath and watch the show unfold.

Chapter 2

THE THUNDEROUS DRUMS OF THE OPENING CRED-
its match the pounding of my heart as the screen lights up with
the opening credits of *Fated Destiny*. I've heard the theme song
before, but I never realized how anxiety-provoking the epic
orchestral song is until now. The flute solo, which seemed
beautiful before, now sounds shrill in my ears. And the harp-
like twangs of the gayageum make the hair rise from the back
of my neck.

I watch painted portraits of my costars come to life and
bleed into short clips of footage in time with the music. When
my face appears, Mom and Dad clap enthusiastically, making
me smile. Thankfully, they don't seem like they find the opening unpleasant at all.

Probably just my nerves, I think.

Hopefully my parents' energy will last for the entire episode.

Once the credits show all of the main cast members, the screen fades into a shot of Bryan and me staring lovingly at each other from across the lake at the Royal Palace. I still remember how cold it was when we shot that moment, but I'm glad it turned out to be the perfect closer to the opening credits.

I write a quick tweet to my followers. **Hope everyone enjoys the premiere!**

As I'm typing, messages of congratulations from my classmates pop up on the top of my screen. One of the perks of going to a performing arts high school where lots of kids are actors and singers working in the industry like me is that I can take a break from normal classes when I'm working on a show. But the other really great perk is the community. My classmates and I have this tradition where we all watch everyone's shows and music videos the day they premiere and cheer each other on. I hit send on my tweet and make a mental note to thank everyone at the end of the show.

Before I put my phone away, I scroll through the notifications and find myself looking for Minjee's name. But of course, she's not there. Why would she watch *Fated Destiny* and cheer me on when I landed the lead part in the show and she didn't?

Park Minjee was the first friend I made when I moved to Seoul. We'd always hang out after class, even though, onstage, we were fierce rivals, always vying for lead roles in school plays. With how competitive we were with each other, everyone thought we were mortal enemies, but that couldn't have been farther from the truth. We were best friends. That is, until I started *Fated Destiny.*

Mom laughs, bringing my attention back to our show's premiere. By then, we're well past the exposition, which introduced Hyun, Bryan's character, as just your regular high school student in Korea. I have to give it to Bryan. For someone who didn't start off as an actor, he is *really* good. Whether he's sitting bored in class, daydreaming about life after high school, or playing soccer with his friends, Bryan's acting immerses me into Hyun's everyday life.

One of my theater teachers back at school always said that a sure sign of a good actor is when you forget their character isn't a real person at all. I'm definitely experiencing that as I watch Bryan in the show. Even though I know what he's actually like, I find myself smiling and laughing along with my parents as Hyun jokes around with his friends or epically fails to correctly answer the teacher when he gets called on in class.

And then, I'm on-screen, at this point just a female classmate that Hyun has a crush on. It's always wild to see myself on TV. When you're painstakingly filming every scene shot by shot, you only have a vague idea of how your part fits in with other people's takes. And it's so easy to get caught up in that microscopic view when, in reality, you're only one small part of a much bigger thing.

I used to hate watching myself on TV. I'd spot every little thing I'd done wrong. A misplaced step, or a weird inflection of my voice. I'd feel *really* self-conscious. But now, I actually kind of like it. It's nice to see how I fit into the overall show, and how I interact with the other actors. And the more I see myself act, the more I know how to improve.

The episode runs like a typical slice-of-life show until a little over halfway through, when Hyun gets into a car accident. In slow motion and from multiple angles in typical K-drama fashion, the crash plays out on-screen, accompanied by the thunderous music from the opening credits. This time, instead of being nervous about our show, the music makes me anxious about Hyun, even though I know he's going to be okay. As he's escorted to the hospital in the present day, the show goes back in time through different eras of Korean history as Hyun remembers his past lives.

Aside from the TV, our living room is entirely silent. I sneak a glance at my parents to see how they're reacting to the show. They look pretty engrossed, and I breathe a sigh of relief. I worried that the flashbacks were too cheesy in the familiar way that all K-dramas are, but maybe I'm just jaded because I was one of the many actors getting in and out of clothes from different eras of Korean history to create that time-traveling effect.

The rapid montage of scenes stops in the Joseon Dynasty period, where we get our first full glimpse of me in my crown princess robes. Immediately, my phone blows up again. People are tweeting to say how beautiful I look in my hanbok. My parents cheer, too, and I'm glad. No one says I look awkward, and no one says I look out of place.

Suck it, imposter syndrome. I scroll through my notifications again.

The episode soon ends on a cliffhanger, a close-up shot of Hyun's shocked eyes as he wakes up back in his hospital room. The credits roll, accompanied by a soulful theme song by IU, and that's it. The premiere's over.

I glance back at my parents and see that they're still staring at the screen. When they notice my gaze on them, though, they immediately turn to look at me.

I wait for them to say something, but there's nothing but silence.

"Well?" I say. Nervous anticipation floods my thoughts. My throat feels like it's closing up as I wait for my parents to say something, *anything.*

Mom, of course, is the first to speak. Dad doesn't even try to say anything, but he shares Mom's concerned look.

"Congratulations on the premiere, honey! That was great!" she says. Her voice comes out so forced that I don't have to be an actress to know she's lying. "How do you feel?"

"Yes," Dad says. "You did a very good job."

I whip my attention back to Dad. Things must be *really* bad if *he's* speaking up.

"Okay, guys, spill," I reply. "Just tell me the truth already. What's wrong?"

Mom and Dad exchange looks, and after a long moment, Mom sighs.

"So, it was great. . . ." she says. "But . . . maybe I'm not understanding things clearly."

"It *was* confusing," Dad pipes in, earning a pointed look from Mom.

"Well, yes," she continues. "That's definitely a problem in and of itself. But other than that . . . Sorry, but how is this show different from that other K-drama about reincarnation that did well last year? And it also reminds me of *Goblin* from several years ago. Do you think *Fated Destiny* will stand out against the other shows airing right now?"

Mom watches more Korean dramas than anyone I know. The entire reason why I got into K-dramas in the first place is because of the many nights we spent watching them together. When it comes to Korean TV, I trust Mom's judgment more than anyone's.

Which is exactly why, instead of feeling offended by Mom's words, I'm absolutely terrified. If Mom caught so many similarities between *Fated Destiny* and other K-dramas, that means that other viewers probably had the same critiques. I definitely noticed a few of the similarities when I first read the script, but I didn't think they were *that* obvious. But maybe the fact that this is my show made me blind to the glaring truth.

When I don't answer her, Mom looks at Dad, who only shrugs. He doesn't normally watch Korean dramas—or much TV at all, really—so it's unsurprising that he's at a loss for words.

I open up my phone. All over social media, people have varied reactions from **Whoa, that was so cool!** to **WTF? This**

show is so bad! No one seems to be agreeing with anyone else, which is both a good and bad thing. Overall, the jury still seems to be out on whether or not the first episode was good.

"I guess it's a bit similar to other shows. . . ." I start. "But I think it'll stand out. A lot of people seem to be excited about it! I'm reading through the social media responses right now."

Mom still looks concerned, but she presses her lips together and gives me a slight nod. "All right, then," she says. "Hopefully it does well in the ratings."

I'm about to go to my room for the night when Mom adds, "Hana, are you keeping up with your classwork? I know things must be hectic right now with the show premiering and everything, but don't forget to turn in your work to your teachers."

"I didn't get much done today because I was too nervous about the premiere, but I should still be on track," I reply. Even though I don't have to attend regular classes while I'm working on a show, I still have to self-study and turn in online assignments to my teachers.

"Good. Get some rest, Hana, you deserve it."

My mom is one of those amazing moms that somehow does it all. Not only does she work hard so we can afford my private performing arts high school's expensive tuition, but she also keeps me on track with everything I do between shoots and classwork. She and Dad are the reason why I would never slack off, no matter how much I sometimes want to.

When I'm lying in bed later that night, I listen to the sound of our upstairs neighbors walking around in their apartment.

When we first moved here from the States, I could hardly sleep at night after living in our quiet little home in Florida. I was used to dull forest sounds like ribbiting frogs and chirping crickets, not sharp noises like yelling, stomping, and laughing. But eventually, I got used to everything and pretty much accepted it as a normal part of life in a Korean apartment.

Tonight, though, I feel extra sensitive to the noises, and I can't shake off a feeling of unease. Our show's reception online seemed generally good, but what if Mom's fears are right? What if our K-drama is just mediocre and will get buried with the rest of the shows coming out in the next few months?

A week ago, when I was still at home because a shoot got delayed, I overheard Mom talking to Dad about how exhausted she was.

"Everything is just so fast-paced here," she'd said. "Things are so different from the way they were when we left in the nineties. It almost seems like a different country."

"I get what you mean," Dad replied. "I never thought I'd say this, but I miss living in America. My work-life balance was a lot better there."

"Have you tried looking for jobs back in the US? If Hana's new show doesn't do well . . . No, it'll do well. I won't jinx it."

"Hana will do great, I'm sure of it."

Well, how about now? I want to ask my parents. But their expressions tonight said everything I need to know.

I want to prove to my parents that all their sacrifices were worth it. I want them to feel like being here in Korea is worthwhile and not just one big waste of time and money.

But how? How can I fix things?

Pressure builds inside my chest as I feel my anxiety threatening to wash over me.

I take a deep breath and slowly let it go.

Worrying about all of that now won't make much of a difference, I remind myself as I pull my comforter over my head. *Besides, tonight was only the first episode.*

Korean dramas air two times a week, so the second episode of *Fated Destiny* comes out tomorrow. And we probably won't get a good idea of the show's performance until after at least the second episode airs.

Shaking all the doubts out of my head, I focus instead on the muffled noises of my neighbors' TV upstairs. Slowly at first and then all at once, I fall asleep as my exhaustion takes over me.

Chapter 3

WHEN I GET ON SET THE NEXT DAY SO WE CAN start filming the fifth episode, things are *not* how I thought they would be.

It's not that I expected a pat on the back or a "Congratulations, everyone, we did it!" but I thought there would at least be some positive vibes since we finally had our show out in the world. Instead, there's chaos. Pure chaos.

"The ratings for the first episode are in, and we're only ranked fifth!"

"Auntie's Sandwiches dropped their sponsorship! I knew we should have had more shots of Bryan eating the sandwich!"

"What do you mean the script for episode six needs to be revised? We have to start shooting it *this week* so we don't fall behind schedule!"

Everywhere I look, someone is screaming about something and running around. It reminds me of the American saying "Running around like headless chickens." I hadn't thought of that very specific image since I moved to Korea, but that's the only way I can describe how people are acting on set this morning.

"Pretty wild, huh?"

I glance behind me to see Bryan standing there with his entourage. He rubs his hands together, and like magic, his assistant immediately hands him a piping hot thermos. I try not to roll my eyes.

"Yeah, what happened?" I ask, although I have a pretty good idea what's going on.

"Apparently the first episode didn't perform as well as we'd hoped *and* we lost one of our top sponsors, along with a few other problems. Hopefully the second episode tonight will perform better, but we'll need to figure out a way to boost viewer interest so we can attract new sponsors."

"Hana! Bryan!"

My eyes widen when I see Mr. Kim, one of the top producers of SBC Studios, heading in our direction. Mr. Kim is one of those fancy business suit–wearing office types that always sits at his desk behind his custom-designed, black-marble stone-carved nameplate, so it's so bizarre to see him walking around outside in the cold like the rest of us. Even with his designer brand parka, he looks just as miserable and cold as I feel.

"I need to speak with you and your teams immediately. Can you come by my office after you are wrapped for the day?"

Instantly, Bryan goes rigid straight and bows at a perfect ninety-degree angle from his waist.

21

"Yes, sir," he says. "At your service."

Suck-up, I think, before also bowing to the producer. It doesn't come as naturally and instinctively for me as it does for native Koreans like Bryan, but luckily, bowing is one of the easier Korean social norms. "Yes, sir," I repeat after Bryan.

Mr. Kim makes a satisfied noise before heading back in the direction he came from.

"I wonder why he wants to see us," says Bryan when Mr. Kim is out of earshot.

I shrug. "No idea. But it must be pretty important for him to come down himself."

"Nah, I think he was here for other production business. My manager mentioned that they're trying to come up with a new strategy to boost views."

Sophia isn't here with me today—I share her with other people since I'm one of the "less famous" clients—so I'm admittedly jealous that Bryan has his own personal manager to keep him informed at all times. I make a mental note to send Sophia a quick update when I can.

"New strategy . . . Sounds ominous," I say.

Bryan raises his eyebrows. "Knowing Mr. Kim, it's probably going to be a game changer, for better or worse. He's a scary dude with wild ideas. Like Park Tae-suk in the K-pop world. They're close friends, I think."

Despite his being my direct lead producer, Mr. Kim is someone I don't know much about, but I *do* know a lot about Mr. Park. Two years ago, Mr. Park created *You're My Shining*

Star, a K-pop competition in the United States, under our company and brought back two American teens to be the next big K-pop stars. My favorite singer was one of them, so I hope it's a good sign that Mr. Kim is friends with Mr. Park.

I really wish he didn't want to meet today, though. From the way things are on set right now, we'll probably wrap late again, and the company office in Sangam-dong, which is where many of the major studio buildings in Seoul are, is in the opposite direction I go to get back home.

Before we shoot our next scene, I text my parents to let them know I'll be home late. Sophia usually has my phone when she's on set with me, but I try to have it on me—on silent, of course—in case of an emergency when she's not.

Hope the meeting goes well! Mom replies. **Let me know if you need me to leave leftovers for you in the fridge.**

My mom really is the best.

I'm also updating Sophia about what went down this morning when Director Cha calls out, "Okay, everyone, please be ready to start shooting again in five minutes! We have a lot of ground to cover today."

Pushing out all other thoughts from my head, I get into character for the next scene.

"You want us to do *what*?"

I'm dog-tired from the long day of shooting, so I hope I misheard what Mr. Kim just said.

Bryan and I are in Mr. Kim's office, along with whoever

from our team could make the meeting. For me, that's Sophia, who was thankfully able to move things around in her schedule to be here with me, while Bryan has his manager and a few others from his team.

"We think it'd be best if you and Bryan-ssi started a romantic relationship," Mr. Kim says diplomatically, like he's some political advisor negotiating an armistice between two warring countries. "Not a real one, of course. But a strategically devised, contract-sanctioned one that'll catch the public's eye. We will spread the word through top international news platforms and ensure that it will make the entertainment headlines."

He spreads his hands out in front of him. "'Top K-Pop Star Bryan Yoon Falls in Love with New, Mysterious Costar Jin Hana.' Just think about how the public will react. Fans from all over the world will tune in to *Fated Destiny* to see how it sparked the romance between you two. And hopefully, seeing you and him as a real couple will encourage people to keep watching the show beyond that as well. After all, you have great on-screen chemistry, so it probably won't be that hard to convince everyone."

Bryan and I lock eyes, and I immediately gag. *Oops.* The sound just comes out of my mouth before I can stop myself.

The room goes silent, other than the sound of someone—Sophia, I think—trying very hard not to laugh. Bryan rolls his eyes and looks the other way.

"Yes," replies Mr. Kim. His lips curl into a smile that doesn't reach his eyes. "Believe it or not, you were cast to be Bryan's love interest because our creative team agreed that you and he share incredible on-screen chemistry. It's quite unfortunate that you two apparently despise each other in real life, but you are an actress for a reason, are you not?"

I look toward Bryan again, only to see that he's staring back at me, too. Granted, since Bryan was definitely ranked in this year's "Top Five Hottest Young K-Pop Stars," there are worse guys to be in a fake relationship with. But I'm *sixteen*. I've never even been in a real relationship. And pretending to date Bryan, someone who I don't actually have feelings for, is the last thing I want to do right now.

I expect Bryan to look just as repulsed by the idea as I am, but he keeps his gaze on me calm and even friendly as he says, "Sure, I'll do it. It sounds like an excellent idea. My team and I will have to set up the formal terms before I officially agree on anything. But if this can help our ratings, I'm in."

Both Bryan and Mr. Kim stare at me with expectant looks. It's then that I realize just how much of a formality this meeting is. I don't have much of a choice. In this industry, guys like Bryan and Mr. Kim get to call all the shots, while girls like me are just expected to follow along.

Even though I hate how underhanded and sneaky this whole thing is, I'd also do anything for the show as long as it means we can get better ratings. Mr. Kim is a top studio executive who's been overseeing internationally popular shows long before I was even born. If anyone knows how to boost our ratings, it would be him.

I think back to how my parents were disappointed with our show's premiere last night. I can't do anything about how the show is written, but what I *can* do is catch the public's attention so people will at least tune in to see us together. And hopefully, that'll be enough to make it so that everyone's hard work and sacrifices don't just go to waste.

"Okay," I say. "I'll give it a try. But I also have to discuss things with my manager first."

I shoot Sophia a look, and she nods.

"Splendid!" says Mr. Kim. "Please forward me a copy of the agreement established by both of your teams once everything is settled."

And that's that. It's obvious from his tone that we're dismissed.

Just one business meeting and suddenly I'm no longer single. Not publicly, anyway. If only it were that easy to date someone in real life!

Once we're out of the office building, I turn to Bryan, expecting him to say something about what just happened. But despite how eager he was when he said he'd date me for the good of the show, he avoids meeting my eyes and walks away.

What a fake jerk-wad, I think.

To avoid fuming over Bryan, I stare up at the shiny blue glass exterior of the studio's headquarters. It's dark outside, but the building shines brilliantly thanks to its countless lights. A few people are still entering and exiting the building. When I first stepped inside this building for my auditions, I thought this was where my dreams would come true. In a way, they did, but definitely not how I thought they would.

As I'm walking to my bus stop, I get this sudden, strong urge to message Minjee. Rivals or not, she was still one of my best friends, and she was the one I could always talk to about how unfairly the industry treats girls like us.

We're still friends on KakaoTalk, the main instant messaging app that everyone uses in Korea. I click on her profile and stare at her picture, a snapshot of the cheap but still cute photo booth picture I took with her. We're both in our sky-blue school uniforms and holding matching victory signs while laughing at some joke that I don't remember anymore. We're so close together that Minjee's long curls are practically enmeshed in my then shoulder-length hair.

I might have forgotten what we were laughing about, but I still remember how warm and happy she made me feel. Whether it was wandering through the streets of Seoul, looking for the best shaved ice places, or helping each other memorize lines for school plays, we always had fun together.

I don't remember who stopped talking first, me or her, but I really miss her. But I don't know how I'd even start up a new conversation. It's just been too long since we last talked for it to not be awkward, no matter what I said. Besides, wouldn't it just sound like bragging if I told her about my problems about the very show that passed her over?

When the bus arrives at my stop, I give up on trying to compose a message and slip the phone back in my pocket. Things may be rough, but that probably doesn't give me an excuse to randomly dig up dead friendships.

I make a mental note to give Sophia a call when I get back home. If she can't help me navigate through this whole situation with Bryan, then no one can.

Chapter 4

"HERE ARE OUR CONDITIONS AS LAID OUT BY MY client and our company," says Ms. Ahn, Bryan's manager. "One, Bryan is still allowed to date other girls as long as he keeps these relationships private and hidden. Two, Bryan and Hana are only obligated to go on a date together once a month. Three, PDA is okay but only to a certain extent and not in a way that infringes on Bryan's manliness."

By the time she reaches the word "manliness," my brain feels like it's melting out of my ears. It's times like these that I wish I *couldn't* understand Korean.

I give Bryan a pointed look. "*These* are your conditions? Seriously? And 'manliness'? What the heck do you even mean by that?"

"I have a reputation to uphold," he explains. "There's a reason why most K-pop stars aren't allowed to date. We're supposed to be in a 'relationship' with our fans and be the manly, sexy, and somehow also cute, perfect boyfriends they've always wanted. If I'm all over another girl, my fans won't like me anymore. Granted, I'm taking a break from the music industry, but I doubt any of us want my fans to drop their support now."

"Wait, so then why did you agree to this whole thing?" I ask. Being a girl in the industry is hard, but it doesn't sound like it's easy for guys, either. "Aren't you afraid your fans will turn against you?"

"Hell yeah. But I trust Mr. Kim's judgment. And our managers'. There's going to be some backlash for sure, but hopefully it'll all be worth it."

We're back in the studio building, in one of the conference rooms where we first did our table reads for the show. Bryan's team is sitting on one side of the table while Sophia sits with me on the other. I'd feel totally outnumbered if it weren't for my absolute trust in Sophia. She spent practically the whole night on the phone with me, going over the terms until everything was exactly the way I wanted it to be.

Sophia shuffles through the documents she prepared for today. Ever the workaholic, she somehow managed to write up a whole contract overnight that runs at least ten pages long.

"And here are our terms," she says in a firm voice. "One, Bryan-ssi is under no circumstance allowed to pressure Hana to do things she is not comfortable with. At this point in time, this means that there is to be minimal PDA. And everything, even the slightest brush of hands, must be done with consent. If we feel as though Hana is being taken advantage of or is otherwise harmed in any way, we have the full right to take legal action."

Bryan raises his eyebrows. "Wow, busting out the big guns early, huh?"

Sophia continues in a matter-of-fact way, "Our company will do everything to make sure Hana is safe. Moving on. Two, Bryan-ssi is to treat Hana with utmost respect and not as though she is one of his groupies."

"Hey," Bryan says with his hands held high. "I'm not some predatory jerk, okay? Just ask the Brybabies."

"The fact that they're called the Brybabies is a crime against humanity," I quip.

Bryan's face reddens, and he looks away as he says, "My fans decided on the name themselves. Who am I to tell them what they can or can't do?"

Well, at least he can see it's cringey. His reaction surprises me, since I thought he'd be all for the name. *Maybe he's not as bad as I thought.*

"Anyway," Sophia cuts in. "If you make a move on Hana without her express consent, we *will* sue. Mind you, Hana is a minor, so the laws against sexual harassment are a lot stricter than they would be if she were an adult. Do we have an understanding?"

Ms. Ahn laughs, which catches me off guard. It's definitely not a reaction I expected.

"*Miss Sophia*," she says in a way that is clearly meant to make fun of Sophia's non-Korean name. I bite my lip so I don't derail the entire conversation by calling her out on her double standards. Bryan uses his English name professionally; why can't Sophia?

"You and your client are so American," Ms. Ahn goes on. "Nothing has even happened yet and you're already threatening to sue. And do I really have to remind you that my client is also a minor? Please do not speak as though my client is an adult offender when he hasn't done anything wrong."

"My apologies. I'm just trying to keep *my* client safe, but I acknowledge I may have sounded a bit too intense about it," Sophia replies with a thin smile. She looks polite, but I know her well enough to know that she's secretly thinking, *I'll end you*. "Harvard Law habits die hard."

It's the age-old alma mater flex, a passive-aggressive Korean tactic that never goes unnoticed, and certainly not now. Every member of Bryan's team immediately looks intimidated as Sophia pushes her glasses up her nose and continues, "But let me just remind you that even minors are charged severely for offenses against other minors."

Ms. Ahn narrows her eyes but doesn't say anything.

"So, do we have an agreement?" Sophia says, glancing back and forth from Bryan to Ms. Ahn.

"Yes, of course," Bryan says, his expression now serious. "I wouldn't even think of harming Hana in the first place. Again, I'm not that kind of guy."

"Or so he says," I mutter.

The moment I say it, I realize it's a mistake.

Ms. Ahn raises her eyebrows. "Is Hana-ssi insinuating that Bryan is a predator? Because that sort of defamation would be grounds for *us* to take legal action."

Sophia shoots me a look before holding her hands out to Ms. Ahn.

"No one is insinuating anything," she says. "We're simply being careful. And we're under mutual agreement that nothing that is discussed here will leave this room unless there is a violation of the terms. Right, Hana-*ssi*?"

"Ssi" is a formal Korean honorific that I hear on a daily basis from people who don't know me well. Sophia normally doesn't use it with me, so the fact that she's using it with me now can only mean one thing: she's *pissed*.

"Yeah," I say. "Sorry."

Sophia and Ms. Ahn continue discussing terms, and no matter how much I try to keep up, most of it goes over my head. My least favorite part of working in the entertainment industry is the legal negotiations, and this is no exception. And the fact that all these laws are in the context of Korean society makes it all the more confusing to me. Luckily, I'd trust Sophia with my life if it ever came down to it.

When they're finally done, Sophia and Ms. Ahn shake hands. Then, Bryan and I shake hands. I'm surprised when I feel that Bryan's hands are just as cold and clammy as mine. Even though today was supposed to be a peaceful meeting, it feels like we just declared war on each other.

"Okay, then, jagiya," Bryan says, calling me the Korean

word for "darling" in the world's cheekiest voice. "Are you ready to do this?"

Two can play at this game, I think. I link my arm with Bryan's and give him a bright, wide grin.

"More than ready," I say with a wink.

Bryan blinks, and then, just as quickly, he recovers. He flashes his perfect, K-pop prince smile as he walks me out of the room.

"Well, then, I'm looking forward to our first date."

By the time I get home that night, I fall into bed, absolutely exhausted. Laying out the terms with Bryan before the shoot today threw off the vibe between us so much that each scene took twice as long as it normally does. We only finished a few scenes by the end of the shooting day, putting us way behind schedule. Director Cha was furious.

"You kids were fine before!" he kept yelling. "What happened?"

Ask Mr. Kim! I wanted to yell back. But I didn't, for obvious reasons. To minimize the chances of the general public finding out that Bryan's and my "relationship" is fake, both our teams agreed to keep it a secret from the rest of the cast and crew. Film sets are full of gossip already. And gossip almost always leads to press leaks in our very small industry.

I startle awake when there's a knock on the door. I must have fallen asleep.

"Come in!" I groggily say.

Mom comes into my room with a plate of neatly sliced persimmons.

Knocking isn't really a thing in most Korean households, but it's something my family started doing in America and never stopped. I'm glad we didn't because I value my privacy a lot, even within my own family.

"Rough day on set?" Mom asks when she sees my face.

"Kind of." I almost tell her what's going on between Bryan and me but catch myself before I spill. I have no idea how my parents will react to the fake-dating thing. On one hand, I know I should tell them since they'll find out about us "dating" eventually when the news is broadcasted and shared all over the world. But on the other hand, I'm tired and this is a conversation I don't want to have right now.

Even though I felt mostly sure about at least trying out the plan when I agreed to the whole scheme, the more I think about it, the more I feel uneasy about everything. I *thought* I was making the best choice at the time, but what if I just fell victim to peer pressure and this plan is a very bad idea?

It's enough that I have so many mixed feelings about everything. I don't want to also deal with however Mom responds to it just yet. I settle on a half-truth. "The first two episodes didn't perform as well as we'd hoped, so we're scrambling to figure out ways to boost those ratings."

Mom frowns in a way that I know all too well. It's the expression she has whenever she's thinking "I told you so" but is too nice to say anything.

"Yeah, you and Appa were right," I admit. "I guess our show doesn't stand out enough after all."

"Well, it's only the beginning, honey. I'm sure you can make up for it."

"Hopefully."

Mom gives me a gentle pat on the back.

"I—" I falter, and then forge through. "I overheard you and Appa talking about looking for jobs in America. About how hard it is for you guys here."

Mom's face falls, just a tiny bit, before she re-collects herself. She gives me a reassuring smile. "Nothing is decided yet. Your dad and I are just looking at our options. And this is all for the worst-case scenario, which won't happen! So don't worry. The show just started, honey. You're so smart and talented! I know you'll figure out a way to make this work."

Long after she's gone, I lie in bed in the darkness of my room. Although I always knew that moving back to the US was a possibility, panic and desperation threaten to overwhelm me at the thought.

When I first came to Korea, I missed the quiet peace of Florida beaches and the gentle swaying of giant palm trees. Korea just seemed so loud and crowded and overwhelming. But now, I can't imagine life without the bustling outdoor markets and colorful, busker-filled streets. I can't imagine what things will be like without hectic but sometimes also really magical K-drama sets or the music-and-passion-filled halls of my performing arts school.

Plus, it's unlikely that my parents will let me keep pursuing an acting career if I fail here. And then what'll I do? What will my life even be like without acting?

That's when I make up my mind. I'm going to do everything in my power to make our show succeed. Even if that means convincing the world I'm dating Bryan Yoon.

As if pretending to like him on-screen wasn't enough!

I let out a loud groan and pull the comforter over my head.

Chapter 5

THANKFULLY, THE REST OF THE SHOOTING WEEK goes by smoothly, and we're able to have some time off. For one brief moment, I wake up, stretching leisurely, and feel immensely happy about the first free Saturday I've had in a long time.

But then I remember. Today's the day I'm going on my first date with Bryan.

I sigh and turn over onto my side. I close my eyes, and some part of me naively hopes that the reality of my situation will fade away like a bad dream.

Before I can get too comfortable, though, my phone goes off. I'm not awake enough yet to open my eyes and check who's calling me, so I answer in polite Korean, "Yes?"

"Bryan's team sent over the details for the first date," Sophia immediately says without a hello. "It's at Lotte World, in Songpa-gu. And they want you there by two p.m., when the park is bound to be crowded. They want to make the date as public as possible, and with everyone's excitement, it might get messy. Be ready to get photographed *a lot*. Dress nicely, but also keep it casual and discreet, like you two really are on some private date. Wear a face mask, a hat, et cetera. Keep it modest, and of course, make it designer."

"Nice but not obviously bougie, got it."

I check the time. It's well past noon. I didn't set my alarm last night because we didn't have a shoot today.

I slide off my bed and start going through my closet while Sophia continues telling me more details about the date. Since I'm a firm believer that you can never go wrong with neutral colors, I end up choosing black thermal leggings, a dark gray merino wool sweater dress, and a white down puffer jacket. As finishing touches, I also pick out a light gray cashmere scarf and a black face mask. Winters in Korea are much more brutal than I'm used to in Florida, so honestly, my top priority is that I'm warm. If it weren't for Sophia's advice, I probably wouldn't have even worn a dress in the first place.

I put Sophia on speaker, and she continues while I change, "Hopefully, the netizens will think you two are a good match, but there's still a huge chance that this will all backfire. It depends on how Bryan's fans end up seeing it. From what I know of them, the Brybabies tend to be a pretty volatile and unpredictable fan base. Fans in general tend to go to extremes when they find out their favorite idol is in a relationship. They either abandon the celebrity because they feel betrayed, or they remain loyal to the star but viciously attack the significant other. Sometimes fans *do* passionately ship the couple, like with Hyuna and Dawn . . . but even *that* couple initially got a lot of backlash in Korea despite favorable international opinion. With the Brybabies, Bryan's fans abandoning him is obviously the *least* favorable outcome right now, since that'll definitely hurt *Fated Destiny*'s ratings as well."

I was half asleep when Sophia started talking, but now I'm definitely awake.

"So what you're saying is," I reply, "if this date doesn't go well, I could have an angry, multimillion-person fan base at my throat. And lose most of the viewers of my show."

"Yup, basically."

"Wow, no pressure, huh?"

"Mr. Kim definitely knew the risks going into this, but he must have figured that the potential benefits outweighed the risks. Let's hope he's right."

When I come out of my room, I run into Mom, who's also on her way out. She's holding her grocery bag and wallet like she's headed to the outdoor market.

"Oh, you're leaving, too?" Mom asks. "Are you hanging out with your friends?"

I curse under my breath, trying to decide whether I should lie or tell the truth as we walk to the elevator.

"Hey, Sophia, I have to go," I say. "I'll call you back in a bit."

"Hana, I already—"

I hang up before she can finish her sentence. I'm too preoccupied with figuring out how to tell Mom about everything. I
press the down button for the elevator, look around to check
that no one else is in sight, and then say, "Sort of. . . . I'm
going to Lotte World to have a date with Bryan Yoon. He plays
Hyun in *Fated Destiny*. We're not actually dating, though. It's
just for the PR."

Mom doesn't say anything, and when I sneak a glance up at
her face, she doesn't even look surprised. And then, I realize.

"Sophia already told you about everything, didn't she?" I ask.

Mom smiles apologetically. She also checks that no one else
is around before quietly replying, "Yes. . . . You and Bryan
are both minors. It's not like you can enter into agreements of
this sort without the permission of your legal guardians. I was
just waiting for you to bring it up since it didn't seem like you
wanted to talk about it with me."

I *didn't* want to discuss it with Mom before, but now that I
know *she* knows, a huge weight has been lifted from my chest.
It feels nice to know I have one more person in my corner who
knows the truth.

The elevator arrives, and after we get in and the doors close
in front of us, Mom continues, "Sophia sent me a copy of all
the terms. You're okay with what they agreed on, right?"

I press the button for the first floor. "Yup, Sophia did a
thorough job."

"I thought so, too. And, Hana . . ." Mom takes my hand

and squeezes it. "You know you don't have to go through with this if you don't want to, right? Just because the industry professionals tell you to do something, it doesn't mean you have to do it if you feel uncomfortable with it. And it's not too late to back out now. If you want, I can call the company and say I withdraw my permission to give you an easy out."

It occurs to me that this is the first time someone has really checked in on me to make sure I want to go along with this scheme. I force myself to smile. The last thing I want is for Mom to be worried about me. "Yeah, it's a little awkward, but I'm mostly okay with it. And I already spend most of my day pretending to like Bryan anyway."

Mom laughs, and a little bit of tension leaves her face. "Well, good. I hope you at least have some fun today and all this trouble gives you the results you want it to. Try to make the most of the experience?"

I nod. The elevator arrives at the first floor. Mom gives me a tight hug before we get out.

"Have a good time and stay safe!" she says.

"Thanks, Mom!" I reply. We go opposite ways, and I put on my face mask before stepping outside the building. Because of high levels of pollution, masks are normal in Seoul. But they also happen to be a nice way to make it harder for people to recognize you.

I was planning on taking the bus to the amusement park, but that plan fizzles out the moment I see Bryan's black van waiting in the parking lot.

In a state of wild panic, I look around for signs that anyone else has noticed the van besides me. Normal people in Korea don't just casually own a luxury black SUV, and especially not people who live in apartments like the one my parents and I live in. And sure enough, a small crowd of curious onlookers have already gathered right in front of the building. No way am I getting into Bryan's van while my entire neighborhood watches.

Hey, I text Bryan. **Have you lost your mind? Why did you come all the way to my apartment? How did you even find out where I live?**

Bryan replies almost immediately. **Got your address from the production staff. And why not? I wanted to start off our date with a bang.**

"Wow, do you really think a famous celebrity lives in our apartment?" says one of the ahjummas that are standing in front of me. "I hope it's Hyun Bin. He's so good-looking."

"Why would Hyun Bin live in a crappy apartment like ours? Didn't you hear how well *Crash-Landing onto You* did? Even President Moon watched that show with the First Lady. . . . He's a top star!" replies another ahjumma. "I could have sworn I saw Noh Hong Chul check his mail at one of the apartments the other day. Maybe it's him."

I want to scream.

Everyone is talking about your van, I text Bryan back. **Can you PLEASE leave the apartment complex and park somewhere down the street so I can meet you guys there? I**

don't want people to find out about where I live.

I expect a smart comment back, but a few seconds later, the SUV's engine roars to life and the car slowly pulls away from the parking lot.

"Hm, maybe we missed whoever went in the car," the first ahjumma says, sounding disappointed.

"Or maybe it's just the driver that lives here?"

I wait until the coast is clear before walking across the parking lot, glancing back every few seconds to make sure that no one is following me. I find Bryan's van parked at the curb a few blocks away. When I'm within hearing range, the door slides open and someone sticks out their hand. From the obnoxious way they're waving it, I can only assume that it's Bryan.

When I pop my head into the van, Bryan says, "Why, hello, there."

He's dressed in a sky blue coat tailored to his exact specifications, along with crimson red high-top sneakers. Obviously, his team didn't give him the same "be discreet" memo that Sophia gave me.

Well, at least he has a face mask, I think when I notice the mask tucked in his coat pocket. It's the color of a tomato, but at least it'll obscure his face a bit. Only Bryan Yoon would think of wearing a *bright red* face mask.

Various members of his team also wave and bow their heads at me. Since I'm still standing, I go around and do full bows to everyone, the proper Korean way to greet people. When I'm done, Bryan scoots over and pats the seat beside him.

"You ready to rock these netizens' worlds with our scandalous love affair?" he asks as I settle down into my seat. I roll my eyes as an answer. If I were into Dungeons and Dragons, I would classify him as Chaotic Evil.

"I was thinking . . ." he says after the van pulls onto a main road. "I know you're American and all. But what do you think about calling me Oppa?"

I grimace. "Uh, gross. No thanks. Do I have to call you that?"

Bryan shrugs. "I mean, I *am* older than you. And we're supposed to be dating now, right? It'll be weird for you to *not* call me Oppa, in terms of Korean culture anyway."

There's a part of me that knows he's right. Oppa means "older brother" in Korean, but it's also a general term of respect used by girls when they're addressing a close male friend or boyfriend that's older than them. But there's also an emotional component to the word, since it's meant to be a term of endearment. And right now, Bryan is anything but endearing to me.

I sigh and then tense up.

Bryan waits.

"O—" I cringe. "O—"

Bryan cups his hand to his ear. "Yes?"

"O— Ugh, I can't. Sorry."

Bryan looks disappointed. "Okay, then. We can try it again later. You already said *O*, so all we need to do is get you to say the second syllable. Baby steps!"

It's amazing how optimistic he is.

The drive to Lotte World is slow and agonizing thanks to the traffic. Seoul's subway and bus systems are so well laid out that it's sometimes much faster and more convenient to travel by public transportation. And even the buses have their own lanes, so they're faster than cars in traffic.

Bryan's team probably picked me up to be nice, but I wish they'd let me get to Lotte World myself. Just because Bryan prefers to travel by car doesn't mean I do. I don't say anything out loud, though, because I don't want to be rude.

By the time we walk through the entrance of the amusement park, I'm already worn out.

"Where do you want to go first?" I ask.

Most of Bryan's team stayed behind in the car, but a tall, burly guy that I presume is Bryan's bodyguard is following us at a leisurely pace.

"Do you have any suggestions, Mr. Lee?" Bryan asks the guard.

Mr. Lee just shrugs at him.

"Okay, then." Bryan opens up the map of the park on his phone, and we stare at it.

Lotte World is mostly indoors, with an outdoor "island" area that has the bigger rides like the Viking and the skyscraper-tall Gyro Drop. Overall, the park is pretty small compared to Disney World and Universal Studios, but it has a nicely cozy and cute vibe that none of the large parks back in Florida had.

"Easy, let's go on Pharaoh's Fury," says Bryan. "That'll

have you screaming 'Oppa' for sure."

"A haunted tomb ride? Nice try, but no way I'm going on that ride. I hate scary stuff."

"Fine. How about bumper cars?"

A smile slides onto my face. I've always loved bumper cars, and the mere thought of legally driving into Bryan fills me with mischievous glee. "All right, let's go."

Bryan raises an eyebrow but doesn't say anything.

Thanks to our face masks, we're able to walk through a good portion of the amusement park without anyone recognizing us. Which would be a good thing if we weren't here on a fake date.

"Bryan . . . what if no one notices us?" I ask. "I know we're supposed to look like we're secretly dating around, but . . . do you think we should take off our face masks?"

"Nah." Bryan shakes his head. "If no one notices us, we can just have a fun day at the amusement park. Chill."

The casual way he answers baffles me.

"No, but really. I'm giving up my first free Saturday in a while for this. *We're* giving up our Saturday for this."

Bryan sighs, sounding so exasperated that I snap to attention on his face. Even with the face mask, I can tell from his eyes that something's up. Instead of the playful shine they had just moments before, he looks fatigued in a way that makes me realize that his previous enthusiasm must have been an act.

"People *will* notice," he says. "And they already have. Look."

He runs a hand through his hair with a quick flick of his wrist, and I take that as a sign for me to glance behind us. And sure enough, I spot two middle school–age girls still in their uniforms. They're slowly following us, whispering to each other. Their wide eyes flick away the moment our gazes meet.

"Wow, are those the Brybabies?"

"I think so," he says with a shrug. "A lot of the more committed fans know what I look like even with a face mask on."

"Jeez, that sucks."

Bryan shrugs again. "It's fine. My fans are nice, for the most part. I'm thankful."

"What about the sasaeng fans?"

Bryan stiffens. "They can be a bit creepy, but I don't think they're bad people. . . ."

Sasaeng fans are the scary fans that give K-pop fandom a bad rep because of how stalkerish they are. They're the ones that show up in front of people's houses or go bonkers when they find out that their idols married someone else. Luckily, they only make up a small minority of a largely positive fan base, but stories like that make me glad that I'm an actress and not involved in the K-pop world.

Except now I'm supposedly dating one of K-pop's biggest stars. I don't know how to feel about all this.

Bryan and I don't say anything else to each other when we reach the line for the bumper cars. The rink is small and surrounded by racing-flag-checkered walls and blue and white carnival lights. Kids in school uniforms and a few adults drive around in cute, brightly colored cars.

When it's our turn to enter the rink, I get into a yellow bumper car with black-and-white racing stripes while Bryan gets into a green one. Looking perfectly content, he follows the safety instructions and carefully puts on his seat belt. I do the same.

The moment the ride begins, Bryan steps on his acceleration pedal. His car zips forward.

"Now this is what I'm talking about!" He exclaims with pure unadulterated joy.

His enthusiasm makes me smile. The bumper cars are such a mess—a chaotic whirlwind of fun that feels like a real-life version of *Mario Kart*. They're faster than I thought they'd be, which makes me all the more giddy. Suddenly this date doesn't seem so bad after all.

Someone runs into me with a loud *THWACK*.

"Oops, sorry!"

I turn around just in time to see Bryan driving off with a look in his eyes that's decidedly *not* apologetic. *Of course* it's him.

"Oh no you don't!"

I steer toward him, pressing my foot on the pedal and urging my car to go-go-go-go. I run into Bryan with a satisfying *THUNK*.

"Hah!" I exclaim triumphantly.

But before I can celebrate for too long, the momentum causes Bryan's car to hit the girl behind him.

"I'm so sorry," he says.

Her eyes go wide.

"Omo!" the girl exclaims in surprise. "Bryan Yoon?"

Her phone is out in an instant, and even in the chaos of the spinning cars around us, she manages to snap pictures of Bryan and me. While she's doing that, some other cars come to a stop near us, causing a traffic jam that would have been disastrous if we were in real cars.

"Let's go," Bryan says as he steers his car back toward the entrance.

I follow him, but in the end, neither of us make it out of the bumper car rink in time to escape the onrush of fans.

Chapter 6

WITH MR. LEE ACTING AS A HUMAN SHIELD IN front of us, Bryan and I manage to get out of our cars and exit the bumper car area. But we don't get much farther.

This is it, I think as the fans surround us. *We're trapped.*

I know we're on this date to get noticed, but I still can't stop the waves of anxiety crashing over me. People block our way, snapping pictures and filming us on their phones. And even more nerve-racking is the knowledge that at this very moment, countless people all over the world might be posting and commenting about Bryan and me, saying whatever they want to say. I get an overwhelming urge to check my phone and see what the worst is.

Instead, I exchange a look with Bryan, who nods and steps in front of me.

"Hi, everyone," he says after taking off his face mask. "How are you all doing today?"

At Bryan's direct acknowledgment, several people in the crowd shriek. A general buzz of excitement fills the now claustrophobically packed hallway.

"Unfortunately, I didn't bring any pens with me, so I can't give anyone my autograph, but I really do appreciate your love and support," Bryan says, smiling brightly like the perfect prince the entire world believes him to be.

"I have a pen!" shouts a fan.

"I do too!"

Suddenly, at least a dozen people are holding pens out at us. Bryan shoots me an apologetic look, but I shake my head and say, "Totally fine. Let's sign a couple."

Most people only want signatures from Bryan, but a few people come up to ask me for an autograph, too. I'm shocked and flattered. This is the first time that anyone's ever wanted my signature.

After a while, Bryan grabs my hand.

"Come on," he says.

And then before I can even process what's going on, Bryan and I are dodging and bolting through the crowd, leaving everyone in the dust.

I've seen plenty of scenes in K-dramas where the main characters run away while holding hands. Usually the camera is in slow motion and there's bright, romantic music playing in the background as the couple runs, with somehow flawless hair and makeup.

In real life, my hair's all up in my face as Bryan and I run away from the fans. There's no music, but there is the sound of dozens of fans screaming after Bryan. My heart's pounding in my ears as I struggle to find a safe place for us to hide in a now packed amusement park.

The crowd only grows larger and louder as it follows after us. Fortunately, after some crafty turns here and there, we manage to lose everyone for the time being. Mr. Lee managed to keep up with us, and the three of us all bend forward with our hands on our knees as we try to catch our breaths.

"Sorry I didn't give you a heads-up," Bryan says. He's smiling, and his face is flushed with exhilaration. He's actually enjoying this. "I just felt like we'd be there forever if we didn't escape. And then this wouldn't be much of a date, would it?"

But this isn't a date, I want to remind him. *Not a real one, anyway.* Instead, I change the subject. "Okay, where to next? I kind of want to go to a ride that minimizes the number of pictures that people can take of us. I know the whole point of this date is so people can see us together, but I could use a breather. I don't want to be ambushed like that again."

"Hm." Bryan rests his head on his hand in a contemplative gesture for a few seconds before his face lights up. "How about a fast ride? Like a roller coaster?"

"Not exactly what I had in mind, but sure?"

"Look," he says, pointing. "You see that spiraling sky-blue rail that snakes around the park?"

I follow his finger and notice for the first time that at the far edges of the park, there's a roller-coaster rail that snakes and hugs the park's walls as it twists around and around and goes through several tunnels. As I'm staring at it, a roller-coaster car goes speeding across with people screaming at the top of their lungs.

My heart starts beating faster just at the sight of the roller coaster. The last time I'd gone on one was at Universal Studios in Orlando back when we lived in Florida. I don't know if I still have the stomach for them, but I used to love them as a kid. And I'm more excited than anything to try riding one now.

Bryan must have mistaken my silence as fear because he smirks and says, "If you're too chicken to ride it, then don't worry about it. We can just go on the merry-go-round or something—"

"Nah," I cut him off. "Let's go. The person who screams the most has to buy the other one a stuffed animal."

A laugh escapes from Bryan's lips, sounding like a sharp bark. "Hah! Okay, it's on."

"How are we supposed to get on it, though?" I wonder out loud. "The roller coaster is past the crowd of fans."

Bryan has a thoughtful look on his face again before he says, "I got it."

And that's all the warning Mr. Lee and I get before Bryan starts bolting back in the direction we came from.

"What?" I exclaim. "Have you lost your mind?"

Mr. Lee makes an equally baffled noise as he runs after Bryan.

"Just trust me!" Bryan calls back.

Wondering if all of this is a terrible idea, I follow Bryan, right into the crowd of screaming fans.

For one confusing moment, I think Bryan's going to run right into the Brybabies. The fans must have had the same thought because they all get out of the way.

But at the very last second, Bryan sharply turns right, whizzing past everyone.

After a few seconds of looking dazed and perplexed, the fans all start screaming and chasing after him, leaving me alone like I'm suddenly invisible. I don't know whether to be thankful for Bryan or afraid of him. This guy really is something else.

I slow down to jog after the crowd at a leisurely pace, catching my breath as Bryan pivots and runs to the roller coaster. Once he reaches the line, he bows and strikes up a conversation with the people standing in front of him. I'm too far away to hear what he's saying, but I can tell from the way he's bowing rapidly and smiling that he's working his charm.

I speed up until I'm close enough to hear what's going on. By then, he's almost at the very front.

"Thank you so much for letting me cut to the front of the line," I hear him say. "You really didn't have to. I was perfectly happy with standing in line! If you'd like, I'd love to make it up to you by taking a selfie with you or giving you an autograph."

Everyone cheers, and Bryan gets busy smiling at people's phones and signing whatever they ask him to sign. Just looking at him work is both amazing and exhausting. Bryan is many things, but he's definitely a pro at fan service.

By the time I catch up to him, we're far enough into the line of people that the crowd can't get to us. After a short wait, we sit at the front of the roller coaster.

A worker comes to pull down the safety belt over our heads, while another one instructs everyone to store all bags, phones, and other things that can fly out during the ride in the nearby cubbies.

Bryan gives me a little nudge.

"Ready to scream your head off?" he asks.

I don't deem that worthy of a response. Instead, I just smile. Little does Bryan know that Kid Me was obsessed with roller coasters. Growing up near Orlando means that I always had easy access to all kinds of different rides. In the end, I had to stop going on roller coasters for the sake of my dad, who kept getting sick from having to go on them with me all the time.

Although I have no way of knowing how my body's going to react to roller coasters now, I'm buzzing with excitement at the sheer fact that I'm currently sitting in one.

The ride slowly begins to move, and the conversations around us die down to a low murmur as people wait in anticipation.

"You ready to buy me a stuffed animal?" Bryan whispers as the roller coaster picks up speed, climbing higher and higher up the rail. "Here we go!"

That's the last thing I hear Bryan say before the ride drops down at a speed so fast that the wind gets knocked out of my lungs. Some people—Bryan included—yell, but I can't get a single sound out as the ride spins around and around at an unbelievable pace.

I feel every twist in the bottom of my stomach and my eyes tear up from the wind. But instead of being afraid, I'm ecstatic. The super speed of the roller coaster is so freeing. The suspension of gravity, exhilarating. I feel like I'm flying. And the best part? No one can reach us. I'm totally isolated on this roller coaster, literally going too fast for anyone to get a clear view of us or comment on my business.

I can't remember the last time I've been this happy. I feel so *alive*.

"Aw yeah!" I shout at the next drop.

I'm so caught up in my own joy that I forget Bryan's still sitting there beside me until the ride's almost over. He's absolutely silent, and we're going through a dark tunnel, so I can't see his face.

"Bryan, you okay?" I yell as loud as I can above the roar of the roller coaster.

No response.

I'm wondering if Bryan has passed out when, suddenly, I

feel a squeeze on my arm.

Our roller coaster hurtles out of the tunnel, going up and down for one last spin. Bryan's face is white as a sheet as he tightens his grip on me. He's literally clutching my arm for dear life.

He screams, and I'm reminded that he sings all the high parts in his boy band's songs. He's not much of an "angelic voice" now, but I can definitely hear the range.

I'm starting to lose circulation in my arm. I would have minded if his reaction weren't totally hilarious.

Bryan seems terrified, though, so I try my best to not laugh. I may not be his biggest fan, but I still let him hold my arm for the rest of the ride.

When we finally come to a stop, Bryan doesn't get up.

"Um . . . you okay?" I ask.

At the sound of my voice, he slowly turns to look at me. His eyes are wide and kind of glazed, like he's stunned.

"Hello?" I try again.

Bryan snaps to attention, his gaze immediately focusing on me. "How can you be perfectly fine after that ride?"

I finally lose it, giggling so hard that I can barely breathe. "It made my stomach churn a bit, but I thought it was really fun! I freakin' love roller coasters."

Bryan groans. "Ugh, I wish I'd known that sooner. You were acting like you were scared earlier! I'm going to be sick."

"It *has* been a long time since I've ridden one," I explain. "I wasn't sure if I'd still like it."

I gently help him out of his seat. By that point, a small crowd's begun to gather around us, only deterred by the ride workers who are doing their best to usher everyone out of the disembarking area.

Mr. Lee steps in front of us so the fans can't get a good picture of Bryan in his current state. I shift my weight a little so I'm blocking people's view of him, too. No one deserves to have photos taken of them when they're about to lose their lunch.

"Here, I'll help you find the restroom," I say.

With Mr. Lee's help, I navigate Bryan to the bathrooms. Thankfully, Bryan doesn't throw up—not that I could hear, anyway—but he doesn't come out for a long time. When he finally does, his face and hair are a bit wet, like he splashed water on himself.

"I am never getting on another roller coaster ever again," he says. "Especially not with you."

"Was that your first time on a roller coaster?" I ask innocently.

"No, but it's been a long time for me, too. Maybe it's all the twists or the advances in technology or *something*, but whatever it was, that ride was a lot scarier than I thought it would be. I feel like my stomach got dislodged."

I give Bryan my best sympathetic look. But I don't dare say anything out loud, in case a joke or jab slips out. It's hard not

59

to gloat when Bryan was so obnoxious before.

"Okay, okay," he says. "Let's go get you your stuffed animal."

"What? Oh, we don't have to," I reply, completely thrown off by the fact that he remembered.

"Nah, fair is fair."

It doesn't feel right to get a prize when the ride made him sick. I'm about to protest again when he winks and adds, "Don't worry, Oppa will buy it for you."

And that's when I decide to pick the most expensive stuffed animal in the store.

Chapter 7

WE LEAVE THE GIFT SHOP WITH A HUGE TEDDY bear that's almost as big as I am. I've managed to perch it on my shoulders, but Bryan has to keep his hand on its back so it doesn't fall off.

"You couldn't have chosen a smaller bear, huh," Bryan grumbles.

"Hey, you never said the doll had to be a reasonable size. Besides, you're an internationally famous K-pop star. Wouldn't you look cheap to your fans if you didn't buy me an impressive gift?"

Bryan sighs. "Fair."

I was expecting a smart comeback, but he looks worn out and still a little green from the roller coaster. He must be exhausted, despite how much he's trying to hide it. I pause in my gloating to ask, "Hey, seriously, are you okay? Want to call it a day?"

Bryan shakes his head and forces a smirk. "You can't get rid of me that easily. Let's just do something chill for the rest of this date, though."

I'm about to ask Bryan what he wants to do next when he cocks a thumb in the teddy bear's direction.

"So, what are you going to name the bear?"

Before I can answer, he adds, "You should name it Bryan because I bought him."

I narrow my eyes at him. "What kind of guy tells a girl to name her bear after him? Wouldn't that be kind of creepy?"

Bryan heaves a sigh. This time, it's exaggerated enough that I know he's just being dramatic. "Fine. You pick a name, then. I was kidding."

"Uh-huh. . . . Well, with or without your permission, I'm going to name the bear Theodore."

"Theodore?" Bryan repeats slowly, sounding out all the vowels.

"Yup! It's the formal version of Teddy," I reply. "And Teddy is way too commonplace for this bear. So, Theodore!"

"That's fair. Theodore. What a very American name. I like it!"

I beam and then stop myself. Since when did Bryan's approval make me *happy*?

It's because of the bear, I tell myself. *The bear is cute, so it made you happy, not him.*

"So . . ." I say, wanting to change the subject. "Where to

next? You said you wanted to do something more chill, right?"

"Yeah." Bryan shudders. "I don't want to actually throw up."

A smug smile forms on my lips. "How about the merry-go-round?" I ask, thinking back to how he teased me with that very option just an hour or so ago.

Bryan shoots me a glare, but then his expression eases into a smile, too.

"Sounds good. Let's go."

Despite Bryan's charm and persistence, the attendant at the ride refuses to let us take the huge teddy bear with us, saying that it'd be a huge safety hazard. So we leave Theodore with Mr. Lee—who doesn't look very happy with the turn of events—while we get on the ride.

The amusement park's security staff, who must have finally gotten word that Bryan and I are at the park, prevents anyone from getting on the ride with us, but I can still see the fans taking videos and photos of us from behind the fence. The small crowd watches our every move as we go around and around on the horses, and I try my best to have a good time.

I shoot furtive glances in Bryan's direction, checking to see if he's okay. At first, he still looks a little pale, but as the ride progresses, he visibly relaxes.

Bit by bit, and despite the countless pairs of eyes staring at us, I find myself relaxing, too. And I can't help but smile whenever we pass Mr. Lee and see him just standing there, sullenly staring at us with Theodore on his shoulders.

Despite its ups and downs, today turned out to be not so bad. I get off the merry-go-round feeling a whole lot lighter than I felt before getting on it.

At the end of our "date," Bryan holds out a bag to me.

"Here," he says. "One of my team members bought us new clothes so we could sneak out of the park in relative peace. People probably have plenty of pictures of us by now. No need to entertain them until the very end."

I definitely see the logic in that. Bryan and I sneak into the restrooms to change.

As I'm switching clothes, I briefly consider dressing up Theodore before ultimately deciding against it. Fortunately, enough people are carrying around gigantic teddy bears that he won't stick out too much.

After I'm done, I wait for a few minutes so Bryan and I won't come out of the restrooms at the same time. Even with new clothes, it'd be far more conspicuous if we walked out together.

Okay, Bryan texts me. **You can come out now.**

It takes me a moment to find Bryan because he's now dressed in a very understated, all-black outfit that is the total opposite of the clown clothes he was wearing before. Meanwhile, I'm dressed in a bright red coat and blue pants. It doesn't escape me that, either by coincidence or someone else's amusement, Bryan and I have basically switched styles.

Bryan ends up carrying Theodore on his back on our way out of the park. The sight of them together is so cute that I pull out my phone to take a picture before I even think about what I'm doing.

At first, Bryan gives me a guarded glare, but slowly, he relaxes.

I'm about to say something when a shout of recognition comes from behind us.

"Welp, these disguises didn't last long at all," Bryan says before we break off into another run.

Seeing him jog with Theodore on his back is just too funny, and I snap quick photos of the dramatic facial expressions Bryan makes while we run.

I laugh, so much that my belly hurts and I almost trip over my own feet.

By the time we slip back into the van, I'm still smiling, feeling way more content than I thought I'd ever feel with Bryan.

Chapter 8

THE NEWS OF OUR DATE BREAKS OUT THAT NIGHT, rapidly circulating in international gossip websites. All the entertainment sites are full of "exclusive, witness-taken" photos and videos of Bryan and me at the amusement park. Some people already posted their own pictures and videos on social media way before any official outlet stories broke, so there are clips of us on Twitter, Instagram, and even TikTok already going viral.

The most popular clips are of Bryan freaking out on the roller coaster—that becomes an instant meme—and of Bryan running from the fans with Theodore on his back. But there are admittedly cute and wholesome pictures of us together trending from our date as well, like Bryan and me looking at each other on the merry-go-round. As I flip through the articles and posts, I'm amazed by how *real* our date seems, even though I know more than anyone else that everything was just pretend.

The netizens' reactions are mixed, even more so among the Brybabies. Some say that we're a "match made in heaven" and are "fated to be together." But for every person who loves us as a couple, there are just as many who are mad about Bryan dating me. Someone even starts a hashtag on Twitter that says **#HowCouldYouBryan** and people list their grievances about how Bryan betrayed them by dating me instead of committing himself to his fans.

I thought K-pop stars weren't allowed to date???? tweets one angry fan. **What is going on with Bryan's management company? #HowCouldYouBryan**

I cringe upon reading that comment because I know Bryan and many other K-pop stars aren't technically allowed to formally get into a relationship . . . of their own choice. It's a sadly common rule in the industry, and I know a lot of people from my school who sneak around and keep their relationships a secret because of it.

But even worse is the hatred that people have toward me.

"Who even *is* Jin Hana, anyway?" one European fan asks in an angry YouTube clip. "Isn't she some nobody from America? I know she's costarring in that K-drama with him, but really? Our Bryan deserves better. She isn't even that pretty!"

The comments on that video are, as they usually are, a lot worse.

Yeah, she should just go die, says one of them.

Die and leave our Bryan alone!!!

JUST DIE!!!

I always heard about people telling celebrities to go die, but this is the first time I've had such anger directed toward me. These people don't even know who I am. Not really, anyway. If they were reacting like this because they hated my acting, I'd at least know how to react. But they're being like this because of who I'm *supposedly* dating and *not* because of who I am . . . so it all just feels very disturbing.

It also bothers the heck out of me how *I'm* the one getting the "go die" comments when it's *Bryan* that everyone's disappointed in. Why should I get the brunt of their attacks when most of Bryan's fans don't even know who I am? Infuriatingly enough, most of this hate is coming from other *girls*. All of this is so incredibly sexist and misogynistic that I want to scream.

After emotionally eating an unhealthy amount of Flamin' Hot Cheetos, I get so caught up in reading through online reactions that I end up not falling asleep until four a.m. I snooze through my alarm and jolt awake at the sound of my phone ringing, my fingers still covered in red Cheetos dust.

"Hana, where are you?" Sophia asks when I pick up. "Do you know what time it is? Director Cha is *furious!*"

Of course I'd be late on the one day this week she's visiting me on set. In a whirlwind of panic, I hang up the phone, send a quick text to Sophia telling her I'm on my way, and throw myself into the shower.

When I finally stumble onto set an hour later, Sophia raises her eyebrows at me.

"Sorry," I mumble. "Rough night."

"I saw." Even without me having to explain, her tone's much softer than I thought it would be.

"I've read so many death threats and curses directed toward me that some part of me is wondering how I'm still alive."

Sophia sighs. "Well, just look at it this way. The show just needs their attention, not their approval. I haven't heard any negative feedback from the studio so far, so I think things are still going according to plan. And I can guarantee you that some people will start watching *Fated Destiny* now just out of morbid curiosity about your relationship with Bryan. Even hate watches are viewership numbers at the end of the day."

Sophia's right on all counts, but I can't shake off how disoriented I feel. My brain's still trying to process how so many people can hate me when they don't know a single thing about who I am.

"Plus," Sophia continues, "it's a good thing your relationship with Bryan isn't real. All this hate would feel a lot worse if it were. But since it isn't, consider all of this as part of the job and don't take any of it personally."

"But what about the death threats? I can't just ignore all those comments."

"Unfortunately, 'go die' is a pretty common Korean insult. If they become severe or if someone posts defaming content, we will report them to the police. Korea has an anti-defamation law that can punish people if they spread rumors or reveal information that is harmful to you and your reputation, but unfortunately there's no specific law against generic comments."

This doesn't sit well with me, but there's really nothing I can do. In the end, I deal with it like how I deal with everything else: I push it down deep inside me and focus on being Sora, my character, and not Hana Jin.

Later that night, I'm reviewing the script for the next episode we're going to shoot when I get a KakaoTalk notification. I expect it to be my parents, or even Bryan. But instead, it's Minjee.

When I see her name pop up on my screen, I do a double take. Why would Minjee be texting me now after all this time? Since KakaoTalk tells people when you've seen their messages, I scrutinize the message notification instead of swiping into the app.

Hey, I heard about everything going on with you . . .

Unfortunately, the notification cuts off her message there.

Heard about what? I wonder. Finally giving in to my curiosity, I swipe to read the full message.

Hey, I heard about everything going on with you and Bryan, it says in English. **And I saw all the comments. Hope you're doing okay. Always here to talk if you need.**

Compared to how wild and ecstatic our conversations were back when we used to talk regularly, Minjee's newest message seems cold and impersonal. But even so, I can't help but be touched that she's reaching out all the same.

My desperation for a sympathetic ear cuts through all pretenses of keeping things professional.

Hey, thanks for reaching out, I reply in Korean. Minjee's English is amazing compared to the fact that she's lived in Seoul her whole life, but I know Korean is still easier for her. **Honestly, I've really been struggling. But I'm hoping it'll all blow over soon. How have you been?**

I don't expect a response anytime soon, but before I can even put my phone down, it starts ringing with an incoming video call.

Oh crap! I jump out of bed, panicking for a split second before I remember that I can just not accept the call. I *do* want to talk to Minjee, though, if only to catch up with her. So, I quickly tie my hair into a low, loose bun and throw a knit sweater over my tank top.

When I video call her back, Minjee picks up almost right away. She's in her pink silk pajamas with her hair up in curlers. She's still as pretty as always, with her soft lips and large, doe-like eyes.

"Hey," I say softly. "Long time no see."

"Hi," she replies with a small, cautious smile. "Yeah, it's good to see you. Just wanted to check in face-to-face. You look tired, but your skin is somehow still amazing, as usual."

It's a long-running joke between Minjee and me that despite

the fact that she's the one with a twelve-step Korean skin-care regime, I still have better skin out of the two of us. Thank you, genetics.

I laugh. "I appreciate you calling like this. Means a lot."

"No problem. People online can be the worst when they're hiding behind their avatars and usernames. It's also totally unfair how everyone's attacking *you* when Bryan's the one who broke their hearts."

"That's exactly what I was thinking! And it sucks because most of the hatred I'm getting is from other *girls*."

Minjee lets out a sympathetic groan. "Internalized misogyny is the worst."

There's a moment of awkward silence between us before she continues, "But you've been doing really well on the show. I've been watching every episode. You're doing a *lot* better as Sora than I could have ever done."

"Oh, come on," I say. "I'm sure your audition was great, too."

Minjee gives me a mischievous grin. "Hey, I never said I wasn't great. You're just the better Sora."

After months of having to navigate through on-set politics and now the fake-dating lies, Minjee's honesty is refreshing. I laugh, and just like that, it's like we never stopped talking to each other. I tell her about random, awkward moments on set, like when I accidentally walked in on Bryan changing and when I caught Director Cha snoring in his chair between takes. She yells, "No!" and giggles along with my stories, and I'm happy just to be talking with Minjee again.

"So how have you been?" I ask.

"Oh, you know. Modeling for some ads, auditioning for shows, trying to keep up with homework, the usual."

"How's everyone at school?"

"Pretty much the same. I have to admit, though, school's pretty boring without you. I miss my all-time nemesis."

She says the last bit with a quirky grin, and I don't need a mirror to know I'm smiling at her, too. "What, none of the other girls are at my level?"

"Nope. I wish they were more of a competition like you were. But, eh, it's fine. It's great to see you on the show. And on entertainment headlines! Congrats on the new relationship, by the way. Hope it works out, both off-screen and on-screen."

She says it so genuinely, with no malice at all—because despite our rivalry, that's the kind of friend Minjee really is. Utterly supportive.

But instead of making me feel great, Minjee's words make my stomach plummet to the ground like I'm on the roller coaster again. I've never kept anything big from Minjee before, and even though it's been months since we've freely talked like this, I desperately wish I could tell her that my relationship with Bryan is fake. But, of course, I can't. I try my best to not let the smile fall from my face as I say, "Thanks."

Minjee and I end up talking for almost the entire night,

with her catching me up on all sorts of random things like how one of our old drama teachers is now on maternity leave and how a new cute café opened up a block away from our school.

"We should go sometime when you're attending classes in person again!" Minjee says. "Remember that amazing mango shaved ice we had in Ikseon-dong? They have desserts like that!"

"Oh God, yes! It practically melted in my mouth!"

Minjee and I had a tradition where we'd go out for desserts whenever we got our audition results for school plays. The person who got the role would always pay, sweetening the loss for the loser.

"You were *such* a good Éponine, by the way," I add. "I wasn't even sad that I lost that one."

"Thanks! And you were a good Cosette."

"Eh, she wasn't my top choice, but I did try my best!"

By the time Minjee and I finish talking, my hands are sweaty from holding my phone, my throat is sore, and my upstairs neighbors are stomping around again. But despite all this, I fall asleep instantly with a smile still on my lips.

Chapter 9

JUST LIKE SOPHIA PREDICTED, OUR VIEWERSHIP numbers shoot up for Saturday night's episode. I'm glad that our plan worked, but some part of me can't help but wonder if it was all worth it. If people weren't paying attention to me after watching the first two episodes of the show, they definitely are now. I could just be paranoid, but I swear more and more people have been staring at me while I ride the bus.

On one hand, all this attention is nice. This is what I've always wanted, after all, isn't it? To be "recognized" as a celebrity. And although I have caught a few fans glaring at me from time to time, most of the people I've actually interacted with have been really nice, at least to my face. Fans of the show—okay, mostly of Bryan—occasionally stop me on the street to ask for autographs. But only because I'm "the girl Bryan Yoon is dating."

On set, I continue my usual routine of burying all my anxieties and feelings deep inside as we shoot our next scenes.

But after a certain point, even that doesn't work. One scene is supposed to be a really easy and quiet classroom moment between Bryan and me in which Sora just says no when Hyun asks whether or not she remembers the past like he does.

But no matter how hard I try, I can't get myself to focus.

After my second missed cue of the day, Director Cha angrily yells, "Cut! Hana-ssi, where is your head right now? Are you going to endanger our entire show with your forgetfulness?"

I wince at his harsh words, but he's right. At the rate I'm messing up, we're going to get dangerously behind schedule again.

"Sorry!" I say with a bow at the crew's general direction. "I'll do my best this time around."

The director lets out a satisfied grunt.

I take a deep breath and focus on Bryan's eyes. They're familiar, and looking at them helps ground me a bit.

Surprisingly, instead of being his usual stuck-up self, Bryan has been giving me a lot of space lately, occasionally even asking me if I'm okay but otherwise only speaking to me when I talk to him. It makes me wonder if he saw the comments and posts about us, too. He probably did.

When he sees me staring at him, he smiles slightly. "Come on, just tell me how hot I am. That shouldn't be too hard, right?"

I roll my eyes, but the atypically gentle tone of his voice doesn't escape me. It's almost as if he said that obnoxious joke to try to get me out of my funk. And admittedly, his usual ridiculousness does help me relax a tiny bit.

Director Cha calls action again. Bryan repeats his line. "Sora-ya, are you really telling me that you don't remember anything? Not even the slightest flash of recognition?"

This time, instead of stumbling over my lines, I give him a sharp look and say, "No, I don't remember."

In reality, my character has known who Hyun is all along, even before he asked her out in the schoolyard. But she's lying to protect Hyun so the evil sorcerer who cursed the two of them in a past life doesn't curse them again. But of course, in good ole angsty K-drama fashion, Hyun doesn't know that. And since Sora is supposed to be a good liar, I put extra venom in my voice.

Bryan puts his acting skills in full throttle, too. His voice actually cracks as he says, "You don't remember *anything*? Not even one of the lifetimes we spent together? Surely all of that can't just be in my imagination. I—"

"I don't know what you're talking about," I say, cutting him off. According to the script, I'm supposed to let him finish, but this feels more natural. And the director doesn't stop me, so I ride the moment as I continue, "You know, with final exams coming up, you should focus on studying instead of wasting my time with your delusional thinking. I have to go."

I storm off, walking through the doorway and down the hall until Director Cha yells, "Cut! That was excellent. Well done, everyone. Let's shoot the same thing again from Sora's point of view."

"Throwing in some ad lib there, huh?" Bryan says when I

walk back to my marker. "Impressive."

He looks genuinely proud of me. I don't know how I'm supposed to respond.

Before I can get too deep into my thoughts, Director Cha yells, "Bryan, Hana, what are you doing? We're ready to go again!"

Later that night, I'm about to collapse into my bed when I get a KakaoTalk message notification. I bolt up, hoping it's Minjee again. But I'm surprised when I see Bryan's name on my screen instead.

Hey, the message starts. **Wanna hang out tomorrow after we're done shooting?**

A mix of confused emotions hits me when I see his text. *Why does he want to hang out again when we already hung out just last week?* I think back to the agreement we both signed, which explicitly stated that he doesn't have to spend more than once a month with me off set. What is he up to now?

Admittedly, some part of me *does* want to hang out with Bryan again. Even though I'm glad we're not actually dating, I did end up having a lot of fun with him at Lotte World. Then I immediately remember how everyone reacted to the last time we hung out, blaming me for "stealing" Bryan. I just started feeling okay again after reading all those hateful posts and comments. I don't want to go through all that again so soon.

My palms grow sweaty just thinking about all the hate I got.

Even if I did feel okay enough to hang out with him again, it's not like I have the time to do so. I've been falling behind on my coursework, and the afternoons we get off early from shooting are usually when I get caught up on everything.

Sorry, I reply. **I have a lot going on right now. Let's just hang out again next month.**

Moving dots appear on my phone screen as Bryan types up a response, but then they disappear, only to reappear. I wait for him to finish and send me a new message, but he never does.

Chapter 10

AS BEAUTIFUL AND ELEGANT AS THEY ARE, HAN-bok are generally pretty uncomfortable, since they have long and poufy double-layered skirts. Since they were hard to get in Florida, I didn't grow up wearing the traditional clothes of my ancestors, so I always feel like an imposter in them, like I'm an American trying to be Korean. But thanks to the power and awesome skills of the costume and makeup ladies, I look like full-fledged Korean royalty by the time I get on set, regardless of how I really feel inside.

When I watched Korean dramas from the comfort of my own home, I always thought the actors and actresses looked so glamorous in their fancy hanbok. But now I know that there's nothing glamorous about acting out a historical part of a Korean drama.

The Gyeongbokgung Royal Palace looks as regal and cool as it always does, and its lake and trees are as picturesque as ever. But I'm freezing, hungry, and tired. Even though the hanbok I'm wearing is designed for winter months, I still need to wear a parka over it when we're not shooting.

My nose runs constantly from the cold, and I carefully dab it with a tissue to avoid ruining my makeup. My breath fogs up the air as I review my lines with the script in one hand and a hot thermos of corn tea in the other. The tea is scalding hot, so I switch hands every few minutes.

Despite the minor discomforts, all of this is just part of a normal shooting day. What's *not* normal is that today, unfortunately, is the day when Bryan and I have to kiss.

But I'm a professional, aren't I? I can handle this.

You've never kissed anyone, though, my brain reminds me. I gulp.

One bad thing about juggling school and an acting career is that I don't have much of a social life. And Korean culture is a lot more chaste than American, so . . . yes, I, Hana Jin, sixteen years old, have never kissed anyone.

In my previous shows, the director let us younger actors "cheat the shot" to make it look like we're kissing people even when we really weren't. But that was before I became the lead. Kiss scenes between main characters in K-dramas are pivotal moments of the whole show and always consist of multiple angles, zoomed-out shots, and intimate close-ups. A swelling ballad love theme usually accompanies the zany cinematography, loudly declaring the characters' love for each other to the whole world. A fake kiss isn't going to cut it.

I know kissing people you barely know is just something

you have to do as an actress, but after our amusement park date, things have been so weird between Bryan and me. We haven't even spoken since our last awkward text conversation.

Bryan gets to the set late, presumably because of traffic. I don't really think much of his tardiness until after he's done with hair and makeup, when he says good morning and bows to everyone except me.

I pretend not to notice. I mind my own business, looking over my lines while continuing to sip on my tea. I really don't want to deal with whatever's going on with him right now.

What annoys me even more than Bryan himself is how everyone's responding to him. Director Cha gave me such a hard time that one instance I was late, but now he's laughing and smiling, saying stuff like, "Ah, it's no problem at all!" and "You were only a few minutes late anyway; no need to apologize."

He was *thirty* minutes late. I suppress the urge to roll my eyes.

Bryan being late doesn't negatively affect me personally, but it hurts our team. We'll have to cram in more work in the same amount of time. Or worse, we'll be behind schedule again. I hate that the director isn't even commenting on how much Bryan is inconveniencing everyone else with his tardiness.

Bryan doesn't meet my eyes for the entire time that the sound tech guy is getting him miked and ready to go. Instead, he tightly clutches his script and keeps his eyes on the paper like his life depends on it, even though it's unlikely that he desperately needs to look over his lines at this point.

Only when we're about to start shooting does Bryan meet my eyes. And when he does, he's a one-man master class in acting. In an instant, he goes from looking friendly and social to being cautious and withdrawn, like I betrayed his trust somehow. Except I didn't. There wasn't any trust to betray in the first place! Was there?

I wish I could check my phone to see if some new story broke out online that might explain his weird behavior. But my phone is safely tucked away in a cabinet with the rest of my clothes. I left it there today because my hanbok doesn't have pockets.

Before I can ask Bryan what's wrong, though, Director Cha says, "All right, you two ready to get started?"

Bryan hands his script to his assistant. I don't have an assistant, and Sophia's not on set with me today, so I quickly run over to put the rest of my stuff in my cabinet.

"Yes, sir," Bryan replies, glancing back at me with that same pensive expression.

Okay, what the crap is going on?

The need to know what's wrong is so strong that it's hard to think of anything else. But I don't want to get yelled at by the director again. I push aside all my concerns and get into character.

I first got into acting as a kid because I love the magic of stepping into someone's shoes. Of not having to care about my own life and my own problems for the few magical minutes after the director calls out, "Action!" When I'm in character, I'm someone else in another time and place, not Hana Jin, newbie teen actress.

Today, though, it takes all my effort to get into Sora's head. No part of me wants to kiss Bryan right now, not when he's being so weird.

I turn around to face the lake, like the script says I should, and wait. Bryan is supposed to start talking first.

And he does, but not in the way I expect him to.

"You're up early, my princess," Bryan says, supposedly in character. The script *definitely* says he's supposed to sound tender and hesitant. He sounds hesitant, all right, but he's also downright resentful.

The director doesn't call it, though, so I keep going, reminding myself over and over again that I'm not Hana, I'm the crown princess who later gets reincarnated as Sora.

"Yes, I wanted to watch the sunrise," I say, inwardly cheering when my voice comes out just as peaceful and friendly as I want it to.

Not Hana, I repeat in my head. *Not Hana.*

I turn around to face Bryan, gracefully and slowly like I'm supposed to. But even my best acting skills aren't enough to hide the shock on my face when I see him full-on glaring at me. Unfortunately for me, the camera is on my face for this shot, so only I can see Bryan's expression. My eyes widen before I can catch myself. *Crap!*

"Cut!" The director says. "Hana-ssi, what was that?"

"I—"

I look at Bryan, but his face is once again a pleasant mask.

Fine, I think. *If this is the game he's going to play, then so be it.*

"Sorry," I say. "I'll try those lines again."

In the next take, I ace it. The director gives his signature satisfied ahjussi grunt, and we do the lines a few more times to get different angles. Unsurprisingly, when it's time for the camera to be on *his* face, Bryan is every bit the doting lover he's supposed to be.

This is why I could never actually date another actor. They are *way* too fake.

Finally, we move on to the hardest part of the scene: the kiss.

Oh God, I think. *Please let us just do this in one take.*

After saying his lines, Bryan angles his head toward mine, making his move. I flutter my eyes closed. When it's time for our lips to meet, I tilt my head . . . and end up kissing something that's definitely not his lips.

"Cut!" yells out Director Cha. "What was that? Why are you kissing his nose?"

Horrified, I open my eyes, only to find myself staring cross-eyed at Bryan's nose. I hear a few giggles and murmurs from the crew. Bryan himself blinks and moves away, looking just as embarrassed as I am.

"I know the script says you're supposed to close your eyes for the kiss, but please make sure you land on the right facial feature." The director groans in exasperation, sounding twenty years older. "Let's try that again."

On the second take, I manage to kiss Bryan on the lips. But Bryan messes up this time, flinching back like he's kissing hot coal.

"Cut!" the director yells. "What was that? You're not the type to get nervous, are you, Bryan-ssi?"

I'm surprised Director Cha is criticizing Bryan. He must be *really* frustrated with us.

"Sorry," Bryan says. "I can try that again."

We go again. This time, I inhale sharply at exactly the wrong moment, causing us to mess up.

"Cut! Again!"

Bryan coughs just as our lips touch.

"Ew!" I jerk back. "You better not be sick."

"I'm not," Bryan curtly replies.

"Cut! Cut! Cut!" The director takes off his baseball cap and throws it on the ground like a disappointed umpire. "Take a break! Come back when you're both ready to take this seriously."

I'm still grossed out by the coughing, so I pull on Bryan's arm. "*You*, come with me."

He thankfully doesn't resist and lets me lead him away.

"What is wrong with you?" I say when we're out of earshot from everyone else. "You've been weird all day. Like, are you okay? Did something happen? Did a new story break out?"

"No," Bryan says. "To all accounts."

"Then what's wrong?"

Bryan doesn't answer. He looks at the ground, like it's suddenly fifty thousand times more interesting than it was just a second ago.

"I don't know," Bryan says. "I guess I'm just too honest of a person to kiss someone who is playing hard to get."

I almost can't believe my ears. *"Hard to get?"*

"You didn't want to hang out yesterday. And you didn't even tell me why."

Bryan looks almost sullen, and it takes all my self-control to not get mad at him.

"Why do I have to give you a *reason*?" I ask. "Besides, you're the one that put in our terms that we only have to go on a date together once a month."

"Yeah, but that was before."

"Before what?"

He looks intently into my eyes, and that's when I realize. We only went on *one* date. And that date wasn't even real! But *Bryan Yoon caught feelings.*

I don't like him back, at least not in that way. But now's probably not the right time and place to tell him this. Not when we're supposed to make out on camera in a few minutes.

I speak slowly, trying to be as placating as I can. "Okay, look. I had a great time on our date. But what happened afterward was really hard for me. All those comments. Death threats. The hashtag HowCouldYouBryan . . . It wasn't easy, okay? Please don't take it personally."

"Oh." Bryan blinks. "Sorry. Yeah, the Brybabies can get a little . . . intense."

"Tell me about it. Fortunately, the ones I've met in person have been nice. So I don't think it's all of them."

"That's a relief."

"Hana! Bryan!" yells Director Cha. "Ready to try again?"

"But yeah," I quickly say, "let's just get this kiss over with, all right? We can talk about everything else later."

Bryan nods and follows me back onto set.

"Did you two get everything sorted out?" the director warily asks when we return.

I give Bryan a pointed look.

"Yes, sir," he says as he gets into position beside me.

"Good."

This time, Bryan's like a whole different person. He not only delivers his lines seamlessly, but when it's time for us to kiss, he reaches over to gently caress my cheek. Even though I don't have romantic feelings for him, the tenderness of his gesture still touches me, and my heart speeds up as he leans closer. Everything feels so natural now, it's hard to believe we had so much trouble with this scene just a couple of minutes before.

"You are so beautiful, my princess." Bryan delivered this line several times before, but now his emotions feel real.

Maybe they are, I think, remembering the way he'd acted just a few minutes ago.

All my thoughts and anxieties crescendo into a feverish pitch as Bryan, like the K-pop prince he is, leans over and kisses me fully on my lips.

Chapter 11

THE EXCITEMENT OVER BRYAN'S AND MY "RELA-tionship" dies down after the next two episodes, and with that, so do our ratings. They don't drop as low as they were before our amusement park date, but they're still pretty bad.

Things must be far worse than I thought, though, because I overhear a production assistant gossiping with an assistant director during one of our breaks.

"Is it true that the director isn't satisfied with the scenes we're shooting?" he asks as he nibbles on some snacks from craft services.

"Shh! No, that's not it at all," the assistant director replies. "The ratings aren't as good as the higher-ups want them to be, so the creative team is looking for more ways to change things up to increase the show's popularity. There's probably going to be a few shifts here and there. Not necessarily all bad ones."

I was in the middle of a school reading on how to best per-form monologues, and I keep my eyes on my paper as I make my way toward them. But the moment I step in their direction, the two immediately stop talking. *Darn.* Acting like I'm just *really* thirsty, I grab a bottle of water from the craft services table and walk away.

Once I'm out of earshot, I take deep breaths. Anxiety looms over me like a colossal wave. I know it's not entirely my fault that the show isn't doing well, but I still can't help but feel bad that we're underperforming. This is my first time being the lead actress. Even though most people are watching the show for Bryan, I can't stop feeling somewhat responsible as the co-lead.

I wish I knew what the assistant director meant by "shifts." I've never liked change, especially when I have no idea what it's going to be.

Sophia doesn't look up from her tablet when I walk over to her. She just holds up my phone so I can check it, which is our usual routine during breaks when she's on set with me.

"I'm not here for my phone right now," I say. "Thanks, though. Have you heard anything about the changes that the higher-ups are making with the show?"

Sophia frowns. "Sorry, I haven't. I'll tell you as soon as I do."

Things stay the same for the next two days. I reluctantly fall back into my regular routine of showing up to set on shooting days and studying at home on our days off. Even at the end of the week, everything seems normal. My parents, who regularly watch *Fated Destiny* whenever they're not working, thankfully seem more invested in the show now. The fact that they care what happens to Hyun and Sora gives me hope that other viewers will, too.

But by Thursday, everything changes.

"Attention, everyone!" says one of the assistant directors when I get on set. "We have the latest revisions of the script for episode ten. There are quite a few new additions to the main storyline with this script, so we will be having a quick script debriefing meeting tomorrow at the Sangam-dong office before we shoot the next episode. Please be sure to have read over the script before tomorrow morning. We'll shoot out a text with more logistical details by the end of today."

There's a mumble of confusion from everyone as she passes out copies of the script. I didn't even know they were making changes to the main storyline, and from the surprised looks on everyone's faces, neither did anyone else. Even though the storyline is bound to change at least a little bit in any live production format, this is the first time we've had a significant change on this show.

When I get my script, I do a double take. There's a new name on the script, right below mine.

Kim Danbi—played by Park Minjee

A sense of betrayal flares up inside me. I've been texting on and off with Minjee ever since our video call, mostly sharing memes and talking about new Korean music, but not once did she mention that she'd be joining the show. Or that she had even auditioned for another role. *But why?* I can't help but wonder. *Why would she keep this a secret from me?* I skim through the script, and the sickening feeling only grows worse. Not only did the creative heads add Minjee to the script without giving us much of a heads-up, but they also changed the whole arc of the show so there's now a love triangle between Minjee's character, Bryan's character, and mine.

A small note in the beginning of the new script explains how Minjee's character fits into the new storyline.

```
Danbi is Hyun's lover in his other lives.
Hyun ended up with Sora for some of his
reincarnated lifetimes, while he ended up
with Danbi in the others. This new and
exciting addition is sure to keep audiences
watching until the very last episode while
they try to guess who Hyun will end up with
in this lifetime!
```

Just like that, Minjee is our third co-lead.

A pit opens up in my stomach. Even greater than the disappointment I feel about Minjee is the one I feel for myself. I can't help but think all of this wouldn't have happened if I'd somehow been a better actress. Maybe if I'd been better at playing Sora, my performance would have captivated more viewers enough to not need another female lead.

The assistant director must have seen the expression on my face, because she comes over to talk to me.

"Hana . . . I'm sorry," she says. "The writers just thought that a love triangle would spice things up a bit. Minjee is joining us tomorrow morning so we can have a table read with her."

"A table read?" I ask.

When we get new editions of the script, we usually don't do table reads because we're already short on time. We only did a table read at the very beginning of the process, before we started shooting. Afterward, we're expected to show up on set having memorized our lines. It's unusual for us to meet up and go over lines together so late into the game.

"Yes. The director wants Minjee to try reading her lines with everyone before she gets in front of the camera. She was runner-up for your role, so I think the company reached out to her right away when this spot opened up."

"When was she officially cast?" I ask, still scrambling to make sense of everything.

"About two weeks ago? I'm not sure, honestly. The decisions were all made above my paygrade. I only found out about them this Monday."

Bryan and I went on our first date almost two weeks ago, on the tenth of December. Why would Mr. Kim and the rest of the higher-ups decide to make this huge change at the same time Bryan and I agreed to his fake-dating scheme? And why didn't Minjee tell me that she was joining the show?

You can't trust anyone in this business. It's something I'd heard one of my classmates say before, and now I wonder if it's true. Despite everything he said, Mr. Kim didn't think Bryan and I were enough to make this show succeed. And even though we've been talking for the last couple of weeks, Minjee couldn't even tell me the major fact that she was joining our show as *my rival*.

Although I was heartbroken when Minjee and I stopped talking, one silver lining in losing my best friend was the fact that my classmates and teachers would stop pitting us against each other. But now we'll have to compete again as co-leads, with millions of viewers tuning in every week.

The next morning, I sit down at the table just as Minjee walks into the conference room.

Everyone in the cast and crew gets up to greet her, bowing profusely. Some people even ask Minjee for an autograph when she walks by them. Minjee's parents are Korean drama royalty, since her dad was one of the first Hallyu stars of the nineties and her mom has been playing the role of the "rich, scandalous housewife" on practically every daytime show since I can remember. Even my dad knows who her parents are, which is saying a lot since he doesn't really watch TV.

Despite all the attention she's getting from everyone else, I stare straight forward, making sure to only watch what's going on with Minjee out of my peripheral vision. Under any other circumstances, I would have said hi and given her a hug, but knowing what I know now, I'm at a total loss about how to interact with her.

I'm determined to ignore Minjee for as long as I can, which proves to be impossible when she stops right beside me.

Since I don't want to create a scene in front of everyone else, I finally look up at her face. Minjee takes off her sunglasses and grins down at me, just as warmly as she did when we video chatted. Only now she looks way different, with her long curls now cut in a short, sleek bob. Compared to how soft and gentle she looked with her bare face and pink pajamas, she's now all dramatic contours and sharp edges with her intense makeup and studded leather jacket.

I'm so shocked by how different she looks that I find myself staring at her, jaw slack, until she meets my gaze.

"Long time no see," she says, giving me a wink. "Have you been well, Hana?"

"Have you been well?" is usually an innocuous Korean greeting in and of itself, but the edge in Minjee's voice makes me wonder if she means it as a threat.

It's so weird seeing Minjee here. And it's even stranger that after all we talked about during our video chat, we've been cast in opposing sides of a love triangle where we're going to have to "fight over" the same guy on-screen. If only we weren't being reunited because of some glorified cat fight.

"I've been great!" Now's definitely not the time to reveal how I'm really feeling. "How about you?"

Minjee shrugs. "Been better, been worse."

Why didn't you tell me you were joining the show? I intently meet her gaze, wishing she could somehow read my mind.

My expression must have given *something* away because Minjee reaches out to squeeze my arm. She briefly leans down, like she's about to say something to me, but doesn't get the chance before Director Cha says, "All right, everyone, let's get started. Since we only have a few scenes to film today, we thought it'd be a good idea to do a table read with Minjee-ssi so she can get a feel for everything before she starts her own scenes. Please feel free to ask me or any of the ADs if you have any other questions."

Bryan, who'd been sitting on the other side of me, gets up and goes around me to pull Minjee's chair out so she can sit.

Since when has he ever been the perfect gentleman? I wonder. Bryan and I have been working for several months now *and* I'm supposedly his fake girlfriend, but he's never once done something like that for me.

If he noticed that Bryan's acting weird, Director Cha doesn't say anything. Instead, he just remarks, "Please turn to page four, when Minjee-ssi's character is first introduced. Bryan, please start us halfway down that page, where Hyun starts talking."

"Sure thing." Bryan begins to read in character. "You look really familiar. Have we met before?"

The question's meant to be genuine and not a pickup line, since Hyun's supposed to recognize Danbi, Minjee's character, from his past lives. Even though he's just reading off the script at this point, Bryan executes the confusion and wonder in his voice perfectly, and Minjee returns his authenticity with believable confusion of her own as she cocks her head to the side and reads, "That seems highly unlikely, considering that I just moved from Busan. Have you ever visited there?"

Even though Minjee is from Seoul, she somehow manages to pull off the twang of a convincing Busan satoori. I feel a spark of jealousy. It takes all my effort and energy just to sound natural in Seoul standard Korean. I can probably pull off a good American Southern accent, but I can't even imagine speaking in different dialects of Korean like Minjee is doing.

Don't let all of this get into your head, I remind myself. *Just because Minjee is a great actress doesn't mean you're not good enough.*

"No, but . . ." Bryan continues.

"Hyun-ah!" I exclaim, since it's my turn to come in. "What are you doing after school today? Do you have plans for this weekend?"

God, she sounds so desperate, I think, feeling bad for my character even as I'm reading my lines. Things were going so well with her and Hyun before this, too. But now he has a whole other love interest more than halfway into the series because people didn't think just Sora alone was interesting enough. Even though my character is not a real person, I feel like I somehow failed her, too.

"Oh, Sora-ya, I'm busy this weekend," Bryan says as Hyun. "I'll see you around?"

"Oh, okay, sure."

If we were acting out the scene, I would have walked away with some of my dignity intact. But since we're all sitting at the same table, I have to just stay there and watch as Bryan and Minjee continue on with their lines.

"If you want, I can show you around the school," Bryan reads. "I know everything must be overwhelming, being at a new school and all that."

"Thanks," responds Minjee. "I'd appreciate that."

I feel really uncomfortable as I watch Bryan and Minjee grin at each other. It's like watching two of my worlds converge in the most unpleasant way.

Despite the whirlwind of thoughts and emotions going on inside my head, I manage to come in naturally for the lines in my next scene. It's a new day, and Sora, having now caught on that Hyun's acting really weird, asks him, "Are you okay? You're a lot quieter today."

Since Sora is supposed to be oblivious to the fact Hyun's even thinking about another girl, I make sure to sound genuinely worried. I won't be helping anyone, least of all myself, if I mess up my lines in this table read.

"Hm? Oh, yeah," Bryan reads. "Sorry. I have a lot on my mind."

We continue down the page, with Bryan and me going back

and forth. I don't have much to work with in this scene, but I still give every line my all without sounding overly dramatic.

"All right, good job, everyone," Director Cha says when we finish the scene, clapping his hands. "The call time for today is at two p.m. We're going to be over at the school again. Hope everyone has a great lunch!"

When we all stand up from our seats to leave, my eyes meet Minjee's. She looks away, and I exit the room.

I am not going to let Sora be left in the dust, I think as I walk down the hall. *She deserves way better than that. I deserve better than that.*

May the best actress win, Minjee.

Chapter 12

I HAVE MOST OF THE NEXT SHOOTING DAY OFF, since it's mainly dedicated to getting Minjee caught up with everything. On one hand, I'm glad I don't have to deal with the chaos of everyone trying to naturally fit Minjee's character into the show—the call sheet for today was a *mess*—but on the other, I feel restless. I'm constantly getting up from my desk to pace around the apartment.

It's Christmas Eve, and Mom has decorations set up in our living room. Our ceiling is too low for a real Christmas tree, but we have a cute fake one set up by our TV. Gold tinsel and round ornaments painted with all nine of Santa's reindeer adorn the tree, and I mournfully stare at Rudolph's face as I think about my current situation.

I hate to admit it, but I'm scared. What if I get left behind on the show?

It's probably just FOMO, I think to myself. *Stop being so paranoid.*

Sophia seems to agree when I tell her what's going on over the phone.

"Just concentrate on your studies for now," she says. "Think of today as a much-needed break from the industry. Get a lot of schoolwork done so you can focus on the show when you need to be on set."

"And when I finish with my work?"

Sophia laughs. "Hana, you're still a kid! Play games on your phone. Watch a K-drama. Read a webtoon . . . or whatever it is teens do these days. Don't let this industry completely suck up what's left of your childhood. And try to relax. Financially, we're fine. You're still billed as lead actress. As far as I know, your character isn't in any danger of being cut from the show. Just keep trying your best, okay?"

I sigh quietly, wishing it were that easy to dispel my fears. "Okay."

Eventually, I manage to focus on my work long enough to finish a decent amount. But hours later, when I'm waiting on set after being done with hair and makeup, I'm tense, my skin buzzing with nerves as I watch everyone run around. We're behind schedule again, so I have to stand behind the camera and watch as Minjee and Bryan hold hands, acting like a couple.

That two-timing player, I think, suddenly furious at Hyun on Sora's behalf. It's always frustrating when a K-drama character ends up being a complete lowlife, and it feels a lot worse when you know that the character wasn't originally written to be such a jerk in the first place.

Dread builds up inside me as I wonder how the audiences back home will react to the turn of events. Will they really be more engaged and caught up in all the drama when Hyun gets himself caught in a love triangle? Or will they end up being disappointed in him like I am? It's such a huge gamble that I'm surprised the higher-ups decided to go through with this plan.

Hopefully they made the right choice, I think.

The entire dynamic of the set feels different, from the way the director addresses us to the way that the other crew members interact with each other.

Stop being so psyched out. I take a deep breath to calm myself down.

I promised myself that I wouldn't let Sora be left behind. And by the time it's finally my turn to be in front of the camera, I'm filled with a calm resolve.

"Wow, how long did they keep you waiting?" Bryan asks me before the camera starts rolling.

I shrug. "Not long. I got a lot of studying done back at home before I came."

Bryan raises his eyebrows at me, but he doesn't say anything.

"All right, we're ready!" announces Director Cha. "Actors, your places."

The scene we're about to film is pretty dramatic, since it's the confrontation scene where Hyun finally gets Sora to admit that she remembers the past like he does.

The moment the camera starts rolling, Bryan, in character, grabs my hand as I turn away. It's the classic backward K-drama hand-grab, one of those clichés that everyone loves to hate but can't resist wishing it'd happen to them in real life. I try my best not to laugh at how cheesy it is.

"Sora," he says. "Just now, the way you looked at me. You remember, don't you?"

The camera focuses on my face. I squeeze my eyes shut, like I really do feel the weight of four centuries pressing down on me. Crying on command is a skill I picked up from one of my theater classes at school, and I'm practically buzzing at the chance to finally put it to use on a show. Some actresses use fake tears—and sometimes, when it's been multiple takes, fake tears are unavoidable—but I'm determined to genuinely cry for at least the first few tries.

My teacher explained that the trick was to imagine all the things in your life that make you sad and play them one after another in a rapid montage in your head. And that's exactly what I do. I think about everything from the long hours that my parents work just so we can keep living here to how lonely and out of place I felt when I first moved to Korea and could barely keep up in my classes. The laughing faces of kids who picked on my "weird" accent—back when I still had one— swim around in my thoughts. And so does the empty dining room table where my parents and I used to have dinner every day together back in the States.

My life in Korea has been far from easy, but what *really* punches me in the gut is the possibility that all this could have been for *nothing*. That, even after several years of trying our best to make it here, my parents and I might have to pack our bags and go back to the States like nothing happened.

Tears trickle down and onto my cheeks.

Bingo.

Bryan looks genuinely taken aback at the fact that I'm actually crying. The rest of the set is entirely silent. Everyone's watching us.

"Sora-ya . . ." Bryan whispers.

"I do remember, okay?" I reply, my voice breaking. "Is that what you want me to say to you? I remember everything. But I didn't tell you because—because . . ."

In my peripheral vision, I catch sight of Minjee staring at us. Her mouth is slightly open, like she's surprised.

I pull away from Bryan and start walking away.

"Kang Sora!" Bryan cries out, stopping me in my tracks. Chills run down my spine. The hair rises from the back of my neck. Nothing feels better than this, than being so completely in the moment with other actors who are putting their all into a scene as much as you are. My skin continues to tingle as he goes on. "Wait. Please, wait. There must be a reason why we remember everything. Why only *us*? Why are we the only ones who remember our past lives? And why did we end up meeting each other again? Out of the billions of people alive on this planet right now?"

I turn on my heel and clench my fists. Bryan's eyes are shining, like he's about to cry, too. He's *really* good.

"Only pain and suffering will come out of dwelling on the past. They killed us to keep us apart before. And they'll do that again without so much as a blink."

The shock on Bryan's face is so genuine that it's like I reached out and slapped him.

I shake my head. "I've said too much. Please, if you really care about me, pretend you don't know me."

When I turn around this time, I make sure my arm is within reach of Bryan so he can grab it. Without missing a beat, he pulls me close to him in a tight but gentle hug. K-drama cliché number two: the backward pull-hug cliffhanger ending.

I turn around, and for four long heartbeats, we stare into each other's eyes before Director Cha yells, "Cut! That was excellent! Let's get in some tighter shots for this scene and then we'll be all set for today."

"Boom," Bryan whispers as we reset to our original positions. He winks at me. "We've still got it."

I smile, more than a little half-heartedly. I'm glad at least one thing stayed the same.

I'm waiting for the bus when someone taps me on the shoulder. Thinking it's a fan, I plaster on a smile and turn around, only to see it's Minjee.

"Hey," she says.

"Hey."

I try my best not to fidget or otherwise appear surprised. Meanwhile, Minjee's shoulders are relaxed, but there's unmistakable tension in her face.

"I just want to apologize," she says after a long moment of silence. "I should have told you about me landing this role. It all happened really fast, and this is a show I very much wanted to be involved in. I should have told you, but honestly, I didn't know how. I know how much this show means to you, too. Are you mad at me?"

The moment she asks me the question, I realize I'm not. Not anymore. Her apology seems genuine, and at the end of the day, none of this is her fault. Mr. Kim and the other higher-ups are the ones that devised this whole mess in the first place. They're the ones who decided that Bryan and I should fake-date *while also* hiring Minjee behind our backs. How can I be angry at her for just following her passion like I am?

"Nah," I say. "I was just caught off guard. I wish you'd told me. Even a quick text would have been nice."

"Yeah . . . I know. It was so nice to be talking to you regularly again. I guess I was afraid to ruin things."

Hearing that Minjee likes chatting with me, too, makes my heart squeeze. But no matter how glad I am we're friends again, I can't ignore our current situation.

"Honestly, I just find it funny and sad that we ended up together again like this," I say. "Acting on opposite sides of a show so people all over the world can watch us fight over the same guy. It's like *Les Misérables* 2.0. Lim-seonsaeng-nim would be *so* proud."

Minjee grins back at me. Mr. Lim was the highly strict drama teacher we had last year who was notorious for making kids cry for "the good of acting." He was into critically acclaimed musicals and highbrow cinema, so he'd probably cringe in pain if he saw that his two top students were acting in a messy, melodramatic love triangle on TV.

"Hey, if that's what the people want," Minjee replies. "Lim-seonsaeng's tastes were really boring anyway."

"True. But is this love triangle really what everyone wants?"

Minjee sighs. "Hopefully. I guess we'll find out when the ratings come out for this episode. This one premieres next Saturday, right?"

I nod at her, my mind whirring to process the fact that Minjee just questioned the writers' decision to bring her onto the show in the first place. I hate love triangles, but if I were in her shoes, I would have seized this opportunity without hesitation. Then again, since her family is practically K-drama royalty, she's not as desperate for roles as I am. That's the big difference between the two of us.

"Well, regardless of whether this whole love triangle thing works or not, I hope you know that I'm obviously going to do my best on the show," Minjee says. "I swear, Bryan and I are just friends. So I promise I won't try to steal him in real life or anything. But in *Fated Destiny*, I'm going to try my best to be the girl that everyone deems to be the better endgame for

Hyun. It's nothing personal. Just business. And I expect you to try your best, too. Give me a run for my money, like you did at school."

Even though I know we're being silly and that our performances probably won't even influence what happens in the actual script, the idea of competing against her in our own secret game is thrilling. Suddenly, all the changes don't seem so scary and big anymore. It feels like we're back in school, just engaging in some friendly competition.

I extend my hand to her.

"May the best actress win," I reply in English, saying out loud what I thought to myself yesterday.

She laughs and exclaims, also in English, "Wow, so American!"

Minjee takes my hand. Despite the cold, her hand feels warm and fits perfectly in mine. Her touch feels a lot nicer than I thought it would, and I squeeze Minjee's hand to hopefully distract her from the fact that I'm blushing.

"How are you so warm?" I exclaim, purposefully being over-the-top. "I feel like I'm constantly dying in this weather."

She laughs. "I guess my body is more used to it since I was born and raised here." She looks down the street. "So, is your bus almost here?"

I was so caught up with our conversation that I totally forgot about my ride home.

"Oh crap!" I exclaim, looking around. Luckily, everyone else is still standing at the stop.

"I think you're good," Minjee says, giving me a thumbs-up.

"Wait," I say, since I can't hide my curiosity anymore. I try to sound as casual as I can when I continue. "So why did you come here to the bus stop? Can't you just ride your car back home?"

Minjee cocks her head to the side.

"I thought it was obvious," she says. "I wanted to catch up with you. We're always so busy on set that it's hard to have a meaningful conversation."

The genuineness in her voice makes me happy. Taking the time to say hello to old friends is Korean etiquette 101, but if she'd truly resented me for landing Sora's part like I once suspected she did, she probably wouldn't have bothered.

"But yeah, I should get going. Have any fun plans for Christmas?" Minjee asks.

"I always spend it with my parents, so we're probably just going to have a quiet night in."

"Oh, that's right, you're really close with your folks."

The small, sad grin on her face reminds me of how much she hated going back home after school.

"The drawback of having famous workaholic parents," she'd always say, "is that they don't have as much time for anything other than their careers. I'm lucky if my folks even acknowledge that I exist!"

"Hey," I say, "you're more than welcome to come over to my place for the holidays. I'm sure my parents won't mind."

Minjee's eyes go wide, growing a bit shiny before she looks away.

"Nah, I'm fine. I really appreciate the offer, though. Hope you have a good Christmas, Hana. Stay warm, okay?"

"Thanks. You too."

I give her a quick hug, and she squeezes me tight before she lets go.

Even though we may still be enemies on-screen, I'm relieved that, in real life, I still have Minjee as a friend.

Chapter 13

CHRISTMAS ISN'T A MAJOR FAMILY HOLIDAY IN Korea like it is in the States, but my parents and I still celebrate it like one. After all the sudden changes that happened on set in the last couple of weeks, I'm relieved for the quiet time I get to spend this weekend at home.

"Hana?" says Mom in the morning, knocking on my door. "Merry Christmas!"

When I open my door, I see that Mom's bought a cute Christmas cake from our neighborhood bakery. Korean cakes are works of art, especially around Christmas, since that's when lots of people buy cake for their friends and family. The one on our table looks like a snow globe, with a "glass" dome made of melted sugar encasing little presents shaped with icing on top. It's hard to believe that all of this is also edible.

"It's an ice cream cake," Mom explains, smiling at my amazed expression. "Dad and I thought you could use a sweet treat after the hard month you had."

My parents are literally the best. I give her and Dad a big hug before we dig in.

Afterward, still buzzing and in high spirits from the sugar, we open presents by the Christmas tree and cuddle up on the sofa watching holiday movies, just like we used to do back in the States. Our apartment doesn't have a fireplace, so Dad sets up his tablet on our coffee table. A continuous loop of a burning fireplace plays on the screen, and with my parents laughing and chatting beside me, I still feel cozy even without the heat of a real fire. Since Mom and Dad are usually busy with work, I'm soaking up every single minute I can spend with them.

Late afternoon, I get two texts. One from Bryan and another from Minjee.

Merry Christmas! reads Bryan's. Short and sweet. I write back with pretty much the same words.

Minjee's message reads, **Hey, wanna go look at the Christmas display at the festival along Cheonggyecheon? No worries if you're busy with family, though.**

Cheonggyecheon is a long stream that runs across central Seoul. Every year, there's some sort of Christmas-themed festival there, where the path is decorated with countless LED lights and other decorations until New Year's. My parents and I went there the first winter we spent in Korea, but we haven't been able to go since then because they're usually too tired from work to deal with the massive crowds.

I bite my lip, trying to decide what to do. I really want to see the lights this year, and I want to hang out with Minjee. She's probably dying to escape her house right now. But I also want to spend as much time as I can with my parents.

Mom, being Mom, notices the tension on my face right away.

"What's wrong, Hana?" she asks, sounding concerned.

"Park Minjee texted me. She asked if I wanted to go look at the lights at Cheonggyechon with her."

"Oh, Minjee! She's your friend from school, right? The one who used to come over all the time."

"Yup, that's her."

When we first became friends in middle school, I was pretty self-conscious about inviting Minjee to our apartment since I knew how much richer her family was than mine, but after enough sleepovers, I stopped caring. Minjee never said anything that made me feel "lesser" than her, and our K-drama binge-watching marathons kept me going when I felt so out of place in my new school.

"Do you *want* to hang out with her?" Mom asks.

"I do," I finally say. "But I also want to stay here with you and Dad. So I'm torn."

"You should go hang out with your friend!" Dad says, surprising both Mom and me. "You almost never hang out with people your age anymore. Your umma and I are always worried. We spent enough time together today. Go out and have fun. I could use some alone time with your umma anyway."

Mom blushes and elbows Dad, making me laugh. I rarely see them being this silly.

"Well, they do say that Christmas is more of a holiday for couples in Korea," I joke, raising my eyebrows.

"Hana, just go," Mom says, her face still red. "Don't stay out too late."

She shoos me away. Dad chuckles.

I grab my coat, gloves, and scarf from my room before heading out the door.

"Have fun!" I exclaim before I leave.

Both Mom and Dad laugh this time, and I still have a smile on my face when I get in the elevator.

Minjee and I agree to meet by the twinkly Christmas tree that's set up in Cheonggye Plaza. Several groups of people stand around the gigantic tree, taking selfies with friends and family. Street food vendors dressed in Santa uniforms hand out hot steamed buns and sweet pancakes. A few people here and there recognize me and point, and I do my best to give everyone I make eye contact with a friendly bow and wave.

Since there are so many people, it takes me a while to find Minjee, but when I do, I smile at what she's wearing. Everyone's dressed in coats of more neutral colors, like brown, black, or white. But Minjee is wearing a bright blue coat and a red Santa hat, an outfit that's impossible to miss.

I wave at her. Her entire face lights up as she walks over to me.

"Hey!" Minjee says. "Glad you could make it out. Merry Christmas!"

"Merry Christmas to you, too! Wanna take a selfie together with the tree?"

"Yeah! It's so pretty this year!"

She takes out a selfie stick, and we take several photos, alternating between various poses that range from goofy to glamorous. It feels like we're back to being just two relatively anonymous high school students instead of costars in one of the most-watched Korean dramas of the year.

"These are so cute!" Minjee exclaims, looking over the pictures on her phone. "Wouldn't it be so funny if we both posted these on Instagram tonight, mere *days* before it's revealed that we're rivals who hate each other on the show?"

"Oh my gosh, let's do it." I smile at the suggestion. "I'll do it if you do."

"Okay, it's happening. I'll send you the photos. Let's do it later, though, when we're back at home. We don't want everyone on the internet to know we're here right now."

"Good call."

We make our way down the stairs to the path along the stream. Compared to the overwhelmingly bright lights of the Christmas tree in the plaza, the ornament- and tree-shaped lights of the path are dimmer but not any less beautiful. Shimmering bridges and Christmas light–covered arches illuminate the path, and tons of gift- and gingerbread house–shaped photo ops line the stream. Most people are too busy taking pictures of their loved ones to notice Minjee and me, so we're able to walk in peace and snap more of our own photos along the way without anyone stopping us to ask for autographs.

Guitarists busk at the edges of the path, and with the holiday music, giddy laughter, and excited chatter of children and couples alike, it really feels like we're walking through a winter wonderland.

The silence between Minjee and me feels comfortable, and I'm more at peace than I've felt in a long time. We spend most of the time looking at the various decorations along the stream, but occasionally our eyes meet. When Minjee grins at me, I feel so happy in a way I can't even begin to understand.

"Hey," Minjee says when we reach the subway station. "Thanks for coming out on a holiday. I know how important family time is to you."

"No problem," I reply. "How have things been for you back at home?"

She shrugs and looks away, staring at a little kid walking by holding both his parents' hands. "The usual. My parents act like we're all as close as their on-screen families when we're out in public, but when we're at home, we're all in our own rooms and hardly talk to each other. We don't even acknowledge each other during mealtimes. We're all just staring at our phones."

I reach out and squeeze Minjee's shoulder. My parents and I don't get to spend much time together nowadays, either, but when we do, we treat every minute like precious gold. I can't even imagine how things must be like for her.

"Well, if you ever want to come over after the shooting day, let me know. My parents aren't always home, but I'm sure they'd love to have you over again whenever they are."

Minjee puts her hand over mine and gives me a surprised but grateful smile.

"Thanks," she says. "I'd really like that."

I'm walking home from the subway station when I get a call from Sophia.

"Hope you had a good Christmas," she says as soon as I pick up. "Sorry for barging in on you on a holiday like this, but I've been talking with Bryan's team throughout the week, and we agreed that you and he should go on another date again this coming Saturday, on New Year's Eve. I know it hasn't quite been a whole month since your first date with Bryan, but last week's ratings were pretty disappointing. And we thought it'd be good for you two to go on another date and announce that you are officially an item since the first episode with Minjee comes out on Saturday as well. It'll hopefully generate more drama and interest to help the ratings."

I don't know what question to ask first. I finally decide on "You talked with Bryan's team throughout the week?"

"Yup, I exchanged numbers with Bryan's manager. We've been texting."

"Oh, okay. And Bryan knows about all of this?"

I wonder if that's why Bryan sent me that random Christmas text earlier today.

"I'm assuming so," Sophia says. "Ms. Ahn is a bit catty and a bit too old-school in her business methods for my tastes, but I don't think she's the type of manager that goes behind her clients' backs."

I think about how much of a confusing whirlwind things have been between Bryan and me for the past couple of weeks. Sure, he seemed friendly the last time we were on set, but that was while we were working. I have no idea where things stand between us beyond that.

If Bryan and I were friends, I'd text him right now and ask how he felt about the whole situation. But I don't feel comfortable messaging him anymore, especially not after what happened after our first "date."

I'll ask him in person when we meet up on Saturday, I decide.

"Mr. Kim also agreed that you and Bryan should go on another date this weekend," Sophia adds.

"What is up with him, anyway?" I ask. "Apparently he hired Minjee the same week that Bryan and I went on our first 'date'!"

Sophia lets out a quick breath. "He's definitely a wild card. The way he does things isn't orthodox, but I think he just wanted to have multiple things going on in case one of them didn't pan out. Which makes sense from a business perspective."

"All right," I finally say. "When and where should I meet Bryan?"

"I'll touch base with his team and text you the information. Just warning you, it'll probably be somewhere very public again. More so than last time. They're trying to get as much press and attention as possible."

"Can we make sure that Bryan and I will be safe this time?" I ask. "Not that I felt threatened or anything at Lotte World, but Bryan's one security guard seemed to be really struggling. Plus, we had to spend a lot of time running away from fans."

"Yup. That's definitely something Bryan's team and I have been talking about as well. We'll assign more security personnel. The last thing I want is for you to feel unsafe."

"Okay, thanks, Sophia."

"No problem," she says. "Get some rest, kiddo."

Later that night, I've just posted the cute Christmas pictures of Minjee and me on Instagram when Sophia messages me.

The text reads **Namsan Tower, 1 PM. Saturday, 12/31.**

I groan into a pillow. Namsan Tower is one of the most heavily frequented tourist attractions in Seoul, a spot that's so famous that it's on almost every "Travel to Korea" brochure because of how often it appears in romantic Korean dramas. Couples from all over the world go up to the tower to put a lock on the surrounding fence in hope that securing a lock there will make a relationship last forever.

And then there's Bryan and me. Since it's the tradition, we'll probably be expected to do the lock thing, too. But unlike the other couples, our lock will be nothing but a big fat lie, a memento of a fake relationship that we're putting on just for the press.

I always wondered what the couples who put up the locks do when they break up. Do they come back up to cut them off the fence? Or do they not bother? How many of the locks on the fence are actually painful or forgotten reminders of broken relationships? Just thinking about all the locks on the fence depresses me, so I reopen Instagram.

The first post I see is Minjee's, which has the same photos I just posted myself. I like her post and then flip through the pictures again.

We both look so happy. It feels like they were taken weeks before and not just a few hours ago.

If only I could go up to the tower with Minjee, I find myself thinking. *Then I'd actually have fun instead of feeling like I'm trapped.*

The worst part of all this is that Namsan Tower is on top of a mountain. A quick escape would be impossible, and Bryan and I won't be able to run away. Even if security guards manage to keep the fans and paparazzi at bay, we'll still be stuck up there with all those locks.

Trying not to think any more about the upcoming date with Bryan, I comment on Minjee's post with the eyes emoji, a fire emoji, and a kissy face emoji.

Minjee has over a million followers, and it doesn't take long for several people to like and reply to my comment. Most of them just say something about how we're both really cute, but a few that have also seen my post somehow manage to correctly guess that Minjee's going to come on the show.

I don't confirm their speculations, of course. But I smile.

If they only knew what we have in store for them.

Chapter 14

IT'S BELOW FREEZING WHEN I LEAVE MY APART-
ment on New Year's Eve, which puts me in a crabbier mood
than usual as I ride the bus to Namsan Tower. While on the
bus, I can't shake the feeling that someone's watching me.

At first, I think it's just my paranoia. But then I start to
notice things: The man in a brown coat who's been sitting
silently behind me for this entire bus ride. The woman who
has her phone by her ear but is only occasionally talking—way
too infrequently to be having a real conversation with someone. The most tell-tale sign that I'm being followed is the guy
with a DSLR that stares at me while adjusting his lens, occasionally snapping pictures when I look away.

Word must have gotten out that Bryan and I are going on a
date. But how? Did someone tip off the paparazzi?

I send Sophia a text.

**Hey, I think I'm being followed. Do you know if there's
been a leak?**

Dots appear as Sophia types up a message only to disappear again. I wait for a response, but none comes. Knowing her, she must either be busy dealing with one of her other clients or trying to gather more concrete information before she replies to me.

Well, I think. *I guess I'm in this alone for now.*

Sophia said they'd have more security on-site for the actual date, but I hoped I'd also have some peace and quiet by myself beforehand. I guess not.

As the bus approaches the stop at the base of the mountain, I rack my brain for my different transportation options. I was originally going to walk up the trail to the tower, but that's definitely not an option now. Getting tailed by paparazzi as I huff and puff my way up a mountain? No thank you. I can always make a run for it, but that's a worst-case scenario.

There's also a cable car that goes up to the summit, but I'd have to time it right. From the bus stop, I'd have to run to the elevator that goes up to the cable car platform and, once I'm up there, wait in line to buy a ticket before I actually get in a car. Any wrong move and I could end up stuck with the journalists in either the elevator, the line, or the cable car.

I look out the window. We're fast approaching the stop, and then I'll have to somehow get out of the bus and beat everyone to the cable car platform. Unfortunately, the bus is pretty packed, and I'm sitting toward the back.

I probably won't make it, but I have to try.

The moment the bus comes to a stop, I bolt out of my seat, bowing and apologizing to people as I push forward to the front.

"Excuse me! Pardon me! Sorry! Coming through!"

Please . . . please! I get a lot of glares and mean looks, but I pretend not to see them. Elbows and backpacks shove into me as I press on. It gets claustrophobic and I'm gasping for air when finally I reach the sidewalk below.

A loud commotion comes from behind me on the bus.

"Coming through! Coming through!"

"Hey, watch it!"

"Get out of the way!"

I dash forward as fast as I can. I'm almost to the elevator when I hear cameras going off behind me. I curse under my breath and slow down. As desperate as I am to escape, the last thing I want to do is end up on the front page of the entertainment news looking like a hot mess.

Fortunately, the elevator door slides open just as I reach it. A stream of people exits and walks past me. I shift my weight from one foot to another as I wait for everyone to get off. *Come on . . . Come on . . .* Most of the people in the crowd are taller than me, so I can't look over their heads to see how close the journalists are.

As soon as the last person gets off, I push forward so I'm the first to get on the elevator. Aggressively shoving through people like this would be considered really rude back in my quiet Floridian hometown, but here in a bustling capital city like Seoul, it's pretty normal, so no one gives me a second glance.

The more non-journalist people that get in the elevator, the more I find myself relaxing. And when the elevator closes without any of the paparazzi getting on, I breathe a deep sigh of relief.

The elevator is unfortunately see-through, though, so I see the journalists catch up just as we start moving. A few bang the doors of the elevator, earning dirty looks from the other people inside with me.

My heart still pounding in my ears, I watch the paparazzi get smaller and smaller as the elevator slides up to the cable car platform.

When I reach the line for cable car tickets, I see Bryan and two security guards, surrounded by a small but rapidly growing crowd of fans. I've never felt so relieved to see Bryan's face.

"There you are," Bryan says. "I was beginning to wonder if you'd make it. My team reserved a cable car for us so we could go up to the tower in peace. Come on."

Once Bryan and I are alone inside the cable car, I press my forehead against the cold glass wall, watching the snow-covered trees on the mountainside shrink as we slowly move up. I hadn't noticed how fast my heart was beating before now, and I close my eyes for a bit and take a few calming breaths.

I don't know how Bryan and other celebrities can live like this. I know this is something I have to get used to, especially if I want to keep pursuing my career as an actress. But I wish I could have eased more into it first, instead of getting thrown right into the deep end.

"Hey, are you okay?"

I open my eyes to glance back at Bryan, who actually looks worried. Which . . . probably means I look way worse than I thought. I can't decide whether or not I trust him, though, so I shrug and avoid eye contact, glancing past him to take in the view of the city below. From up here, even a city as busy and big as Seoul looks so calm and peaceful, and I feel better the higher up we go.

Bryan doesn't probe. Instead, he turns around to look at the city, too.

"This used to be my favorite thing as a kid," he says. "My parents were either always rushing around, busy with work so they had enough money for all my classes and training, or they were fighting with each other. But they'd never make a scene around other people. So when we got onto this cable car, they'd just quietly stand next to each other and marvel at the view with me. I must have asked if we could come up here at least ten times before they got divorced."

Bryan's sudden confession throws me off guard. Although some members of NOVA are open about their family histories, Bryan is one of the idols that never publicly talks about his past, keeping his background so secret to the point that it's almost like he was manufactured by the K-pop industry. But now I can see why he kept things private.

Divorce is still relatively uncommon in Korea and is seen as taboo. I'd hear so many stories from my school friends about how much their parents hate each other but won't divorce because of the shame they thought it would bring to them and their kids.

Bryan coughs. "Sorry," he says. "No idea why I just told you all that. I blame the view. It's making me sentimental."

"It's okay," I reply. "I'm not judging your family or anything. Is that why you threw yourself into music? To get away from all that?"

Bryan nods. "I just didn't want to be home. Even after the divorce, things didn't get much better. A lot of trainees complained about the long hours and nights away from home, but I never minded. When I was selected for NOVA and had to leave the country for tour and stuff, it was a huge relief."

For the first time, Bryan is letting me see him as a real person, a teenager just like me who has his own crap going on. It's enough to make me feel like I can trust him, if just for this one moment.

"I'm not doing so great," I finally admit, meeting his eyes. "This whole fame thing is really overwhelming . . . which is pretty ironic since starring in a popular K-drama and becoming a household name was basically all I wanted as a kid."

I half expect Bryan to mock me for my naivete, but he gives me a sympathetic look. "Don't worry. You get used to it after a while. Sort of. Okay, not really."

"Is that supposed to make me feel better?"

He shrugs, and we both look away from each other again to stare at the ground below.

"I don't think the anxiety ever goes away," Bryan says, as if he's trying again to comfort me. "I know lots of famous pop stars who still struggle with it and are secretly in therapy or cope in not-so-good ways. Knowing that we're all struggling . . . makes me feel less alone."

What Bryan said does make me feel a bit better, but it also makes me really sad, since it reminds me how much, along with divorce, going to therapy and taking medication to cope with mental illness is also relatively taboo in Korea.

"Lucky for you, though," he adds, "the public doesn't freak out as much over actors and actresses as they do about K-pop idols. Not unless you're like Kim Tae-hee or Hyun Bin."

"Yeah, I guess," I say.

My phone buzzes. It's Sophia, finally replying to my text.

Hana, are you okay? Sorry for the delay. Busy day. I discovered the source of the leak. It wasn't anyone on our team. It looks like Bryan posted on his Instagram story last night that he's going to Namsan Tower. He deleted it a few minutes later but people posted screenshots of it and got the attention of the press.

I blink rapidly, hoping I read the text wrong. But then Sophia sends me a screenshot, which is a pretty unmistakable selfie of Bryan holding up the victory sign with a caption that says, **Going to Namsan Tower with a very special lady tomorrow afternoon!**

Chapter 15

I LOOK UP FROM MY PHONE TO SEE THE PRESENT Bryan peering over my shoulder to look at my screen.

"Um, excuse me?" I jerk my phone away. Whatever sympathy I had for Bryan quickly evaporates as I try to control my emotions.

He slowly stretches out his hands in a gesture of peace and says, "Hana, I'm so sorry."

I think back to how panicked I was as I tried to figure out a way to the tower. About how frantic I was to escape from the paparazzi. Anger rises up inside me and comes out in the low trembling of my voice. "Why would you post something like that? What were you thinking?"

"I thought it'd help us. The whole point of today's date is to get as much attention as possible, right? So I figured, why not let everyone know about it? I thought it'd be okay since our teams were doing their best to secure the area. . . . It didn't occur to me that a big crowd would make it harder for us to get up to the mountain in the first place. My manager called me the moment she saw my story and told me to take it down, so I did. But yes, totally my fault. Won't happen again, I swear. In fact, next time, I'll check in with you personally before I post anything like that."

Next time. Bryan's apology seems genuine enough, but my throat still goes dry at just the mention of another date. I'm not sure if I can even make it through this one, and Bryan's already talking about the possibility of another.

Tell him, I think. I want to be sensitive and wait to tell him I don't share any real romantic feelings for him—especially since he just opened up to me. But it'd be completely unfair of me to go on this date without telling him the truth, especially since I'm pretty sure he actually really likes me.

I glance up at the mountain to see our progress. We're seconds away from the top. I don't have enough time to tell Bryan now.

When we exit the cable car, I'm half expecting to get ambushed. Even though Sophia reassured me that the security would be tighter this time around, I can't entirely shake my fear away.

But fortunately, the only person waiting for us is Mr. Lee.

"Our team contacted the staff of the tower and asked to keep this area off-limits while you make the rest of your way to the tower," he explains when he sees my confused expression. "Seemed like a safety hazard to have a crowd up here waiting on the steep steps. There are a lot of people at the tower itself, though. And we'll remove the blockades once you guys reach the summit."

"Where *is* the tower?" I ask, looking around. "I thought this cable car was supposed to take us to its base."

I had a clear view of Namsan Tower while we were on the cable car, but from where we're standing now, all I see are a bunch of wooden steps and trees.

"The trees are blocking the view of it right now," Bryan explains. "But we're really close. We just have to follow the steps up to the base. It's impossible to miss."

As we head up the trail, I begin seeing clumps of colorful, rusted locks on the fence lining our path. The closer we get to the tower, the more locks I see. Soon, there are so many pink, yellow, and other brightly colored locks that the actual brown wood of the fence is no longer visible. All the heart locks make me super uncomfortable.

"We're almost there," Bryan says. "It's just around this corner."

It's now or never!

I grab Bryan's hand before he can turn the corner.

"Wait, I have to tell you something," I blurt out. "I should have told you this before, but the timing wasn't right. The timing isn't good now, either, but it's only going to get worse the more I wait."

Bryan takes a step back, looking very confused.

I swallow and look down at my shoes. "I don't like you the same way you like me. Or at least, I don't think I do, especially not this early. I actually thought you were really annoying until recently. I do want to be friends, though. If you're up for it."

"Oh," he says with a short laugh. "Okay. Wow, this makes today really awkward then."

"I'm still willing to go through with this fake-dating thing for the good of the show," I add. "But if you don't want to anymore, I'd understand."

Please say you don't want to anymore.

Bryan nods, looking like he's in deep thought.

"Nah," he finally says. "We should still go through with everything. We have to do our best to get as many views as possible."

I try not to show my disappointment.

"Well, if you're sure."

I'm about to turn away when Bryan adds, "Wait. You said it's too early for you to have feelings for me. But that doesn't mean you won't ever get them in the future, right?"

"Huh? I don't think—"

"I guess that's normal. I'm a Leo, so I tend to get attached to people quickly. Maybe you just need more time."

It's like he can't accept the fact that someone doesn't like him. I guess it's not a big surprise that an internationally famous K-pop star like Bryan thinks this way. He's probably used to girls falling at his feet. But still . . .

"Bryan," I try again. "I—"

"Hey, you two," says Mr. Lee, interrupting me as he walks over to where we're standing. I was so caught up with what I was telling Bryan that I hadn't even noticed he'd gone ahead.

Mr. Lee's accompanied by two other guards that must have come down from the summit. "It's showtime. Put on your earplugs before we head up to the tower."

"Earplugs?" I ask, still flustered by Bryan's and my conversation.

Bryan gets out a small pouch from one of his pockets and gives it to me.

"Here," he says. "These are brand-new."

I open the pouch to find two earplugs still in their original packaging. I give Bryan a questioning look.

"You're going to hear a *lot* of screaming."

I immediately put the earplugs in.

Since Namsan Tower is one of the top tourist places in Seoul, the square at its base is always pretty crowded. But it's even more jam-packed now, so much that I can't make out the steps that lead to the tower itself. Paparazzi have their professional cameras and mics ready, while fans carry signs that say everything from *Bryan ♥ Hana* to *Bryan is mine, go die!* My brain swims from all the mixed messages.

At the sight of us, the crowd rushes forward. Mr. Lee and the other guards immediately step in front of us to create a protective shield. The earplugs don't block all the sound, but it muffles everything, so I hear a dull roar rather than ear-splitting shrieks.

Bryan says something, but I can't hear him at all. He must have realized I can't understand him, because he grabs my hand and starts leading me closer to the tower.

When they see us holding hands, the crowd gets impossibly louder, so much that even with the earplugs, my ears start ringing. Out of instinct, I tighten my grip on Bryan's hand. He gives me a startled look, but then his face melts into an almost boyish smile as we push through the crowd. It feels like a moment straight out of a Korean drama, except we're not filming anything right now. And I don't actually like Bryan.

Even though it's freezing out, the full force of everyone squished around us is warming me up. The guards—who are doing their best to keep us safe—are sweating profusely, and so are the fans who are pushing against them in their attempts to get to us. Bryan's hand, which initially felt nice in mine, becomes clammy. Although I can't make out exactly what people are saying, I get hit by some of the spittle from the fans as they yell at us.

The worst part is that there's no end in sight. I can see the tower peeking out from above everyone's heads, but we're so surrounded that I have no way of telling where we are in relation to it. I keep alternating between thinking we're almost there to thinking that I'm just hallucinating it getting closer.

My vision blurs. I'm about to pass out when Bryan lets go of my hand. Panic shoots down my spine before I realize why. We're finally here.

I'm face-to-face with the double-storied glass-walled base

of the tower, which has restaurants and souvenir shops. I remember reading in a travel guide once that Namsan Tower has a bunch of cute statues and other fun areas where you can take pictures with your friends and loved ones. Something tells me that Bryan and I won't have time for any of those things.

Supposedly, you can get a good view of the city below from the tower, but I can't see anything except the expectant faces of the fans surrounding us. We're trapped with the tower behind us and the crowd in front of us.

Bryan gestures at his ears and takes out the earplugs. I do the same, momentarily cupping my ears with my hands so they can adjust to the noise.

Bryan waves. "Hi, everyone!"

Fans scream and jump up and down.

Bryan looks at me and gives me the charming smile that's on K-pop posters all over the world.

We're acting, his expression seems to say. *This is all pretend, so play along.*

And just like that, it's like he's pulled a switch. Regardless of whatever's really going on between Bryan and me, one thing has always been true: we bring out the best in each other, acting wise. And today's no exception. I let my lips spread wide into a fake smile of my own.

Just think of all this as acting practice, I tell myself. It's the only way I can think of getting through the current situation.

"I bet you're all waiting for this." Bryan puts a hand in

his pocket and takes out a bright red heart-shaped lock. The letters *BY* and *HJ*, our initials, are scribbled on it in black Sharpie, along with a plus sign that links us together.

I gasp in delight, like it's the prettiest thing I've ever seen.

The fans' reactions to the lock are a hysterical mix of joy and despair.

Even though I still feel awkward and anxious inside, I manage to look bashful, like I'm excited yet embarrassed to be here in front of everyone.

We start moving again, heading toward the nearest fence. As the crowd shifts to follow us, I finally get glimpses of the city below. Compared to the utter chaos around me, the distant city looks so peaceful and quiet. Even though I know Seoul just *appears* calm from where we're standing, I wish I were down there instead of up here.

It takes a while for us to find an uncovered area in the fence, but when we do, Bryan takes my hand again and gently leads me closer.

"Hana!" he says, yelling my name so it can be heard over the crowd. "Will you be my girlfriend?"

He looks so hopeful, so happy. I know that Bryan is mostly faking everything like I am, but I have a sinking feeling that some part of him isn't acting at all.

Screams erupt all around us, followed by chanting voices. Some of the fans chant, "Do it! Do it! Do it!" while others yell, "Say no! Say no! Say no!" Cameras flash around me.

Entertainment news reporters hold mics in front of me, waiting for my response.

The noes and yeses blend together into a confusing mess of sound. My heart pounds, not because I like Bryan, but because of the pressure I feel from everyone around me.

You already told Bryan your true feelings, I think to myself. *So regardless of how he feels about you, none of this has to be real.*

I take a deep breath. Thinking about how Sora would talk to her reincarnated lover, Hyun, I make my voice go soft and sweet. "Yes, I will."

My voice is barely audible, but everyone reacts instantly. The crowd only gets louder as I take the lock from his hand and secure it into place on the fence.

Even though I can't hear the actual click of the lock, I can hear the sound in my head. And I can't stop thinking about the lock, hanging with finality on the fence, for the remainder of the date.

Chapter 16

THE NEWS ABOUT BRYAN'S AND MY "RELATION-ship" makes entertainment headlines and goes viral later that night, and people freak out even more when Minjee's character makes her first appearance on the show.

New Year's Eve Surprise! Park Minjee enters *Fated Destiny*.
What does this mean for Bryan and Hana's new relationship?

Possible cat fight? Love triangle emerges in *Fated Destiny*!

Which girl will Prince Hyun choose?

I roll my eyes when I see the last headline. Although I'm grateful for the buzz, I kind of really hate what our show has become. From the way people talk about it now, it's like *Fated Destiny* is the Korean teen *Bachelor*.

There's a knock on my door, and I look up to see Mom and Dad standing in the doorway of my room.

"Hana?" Mom says. "Did you want to join in for New Year's celebrations?"

"Yes!" I toss my phone onto my bed. No matter what people are saying about the show, I'm definitely not going to let them make me lose sight of what's really important.

My parents and I usually go to Jongno to see people ring the Bosingak bell at midnight or catch the fireworks at the COEX Center, but this year, we opt to celebrate in our apartment. The last thing I need is more crowds.

With the TV set on the New Year's countdown at Bosingak Pavilion, my parents and I sit on our couch at twenty minutes before midnight.

Mom mutes the audio of the TV. "While we're waiting, let's go around and say our New Year's resolutions." She takes a deep breath and continues, "I'll start. Mine is to take some more time for myself. I have to admit, this year has been really busy for me. And as much as I love doing everything I do, I've been feeling worn down. Maybe I should work fewer hours and take a traditional Korean instrument class instead? I've always wanted to learn how to play the gayageum."

"Umma, please do take some time for yourself," I say. "You don't have to work as hard as you did before I got my role in *Fated Destiny*. I can help pitch in for the bills, too!"

"And let me know if you ever want some more massage vouchers at the Korean spa," Dad adds. "I can always get you some."

"Thank you. Both of you are so sweet." Mom turns to Dad. "What about you, yeobo?"

"I'm hoping to get a raise this year," he replies without any hesitation. "It's hard because the company is always trying to push some of the older employees out to make room for the young people, but my supervisor says he's been really satisfied with my work. So I think that's a good sign."

I squeeze Dad's hands. "I really hope you can get that raise, too."

"Do you have any resolutions for the new year, Hana?" Mom asks me.

I stare at the still muted TV, watching the smiling faces of everyone gathered at the Pavilion. Condensation comes out in small puffs from their mouths, and I feel cold just looking at how bundled up they are. But despite the frigid temperatures, they all look so happy, and the people on-screen excitedly wave their bright white phone lights at the camera. Even without sound, everyone's hope for the new year radiates off the TV. I'd been too busy for the past few months to even think about more than a day at a time, but maybe I should start thinking beyond that.

"I really want to successfully wrap up this show," I say. "And hopefully finish it with good enough ratings to get new opportunities from it."

I turn away from the TV to look at my parents.

"And I want to make you and Appa proud. You guys do so much for me. I don't want all of it to go to waste."

My parents stare back at me, Mom with her eyebrows raised and Dad with his mouth slightly ajar.

"Honey," Mom says, "you do know that no matter what happens, we'll always be proud of you, right?"

"And we definitely don't think anything you do is a waste," Dad adds.

I swallow and look down at my feet, suddenly feeling awkward under my parents' intent gazes. "I know. But I still want to do my best. It's what you deserve."

Dad puts a hand on my shoulder while Mom asks, "But how about *you*, Hana? Are you enjoying the show? Having a lead role like this is what you've always wanted, right?"

I glance back at the TV. News announcers are recounting the events of the past year before the big countdown.

"Things are harder than I thought they'd be," I admit. "And I had to do a lot of things that I didn't think I'd have to do. If I'm being honest, I feel overwhelmed more often than I have fun."

"This is your first lead role for a major show," Mom interjects. "This is huge! It'd be strange if you felt completely at ease. The most you can do is try your best and hopefully also enjoy yourself during the process."

I look at her, realizing she's right. Back on the TV, the cameras are showing the Bosingak bell again. It's almost midnight, and the mayor, an Olympic athlete, and other notable figures line up to strike the bell. I unmute the broadcast, smiling at the enthusiastic commentary explaining how the bell gets rung thirty-three times at midnight, just like how it was rung every morning and evening during the Joseon Dynasty. They tell the story every year, but I never get sick of it. It feels nice to be part of a tradition that goes back many centuries.

"Okay, then. Scratch my old resolution," I say. "I want to enjoy whatever time I have left with this show. *And* try my best."

On TV, everyone's excitement reaches a feverish pitch as the ten-second countdown begins.

"Ten! Nine! Eight!"

Mom pulls me in for a hug. "That's more like it."

"Seven! Six!"

"Here we go!" Dad says.

My parents and I join in, counting down with the people on TV.

"Five! Four! Three! Two! One! Happy New Year!"

Bong! Bong!

The bell rings, welcoming the new year. I think about our resolutions and hold my parents tight.

Chapter 17

THE FOLLOWING MONDAY, EVERYONE IN THE cast and crew congratulates me.

"Ooh," says the assistant director. "A real-life on-set romance. I love it when real-life love blossoms during filming!"

Only Director Cha has a lukewarm response to our relationship news.

"I'm hoping this means I can expect better chemistry between you two!" he remarks. "It is a new year, after all. Let's try our best!"

"You and Bryan look so great together," comments a production assistant. "It truly was 'fated destiny.'"

Everyone chuckles. Even Director Cha and I awkwardly laugh along.

There's a palpable shift in the mood on set today. This past weekend's episodes of *Fated Destiny* premiered at a solid second place in this week's ratings, which is pretty good, considering the fact that we just premiered our tenth episode. Although it's made my personal life a confusing mess, I'm glad the sacrifice was good for *something*.

Even the Brybabies generally reacted positively to our tower date, and apparently some of the people who previously hated me are now convinced that Bryan and I are "obviously meant to be." Fan art and fan photo collages of us together are all over Instagram and Twitter.

I wonder how much of them shipping us has to do with our actual compatibility rather than just how good we look together. After all, Bryan's fans may know a lot about Bryan, but they barely know anything about me. How do they know if Bryan and I are really meant to be? Or any celebrity couple, for that matter?

Thankfully, people on set get over the news of Bryan's and my "relationship" pretty fast, since we're on yet another tight schedule. Today, I'm supposed to shoot a few scenes with Minjee, which is a welcome distraction from everything. According to Director Cha, they're "simple flashback scenes" meant to establish the fact that Sora and Danbi were enemies in their past lives.

But the moment I see Minjee in her hanbok, the scenes become more than just "simple" to me.

Everything from the long, scarlet skirt to the elegant flowers embroidered on her yellow blouse looks perfect on Minjee, and so do her rosy-pink-painted lips and thick, long lashes. With the help of extensions, Minjee's hair is now luxurious and long, styled into a braid that goes down to her waist. My eyes linger at the delicate, round ornamental hairpin sitting on top of her head like a small blooming flower.

She looks so stunning and so totally different than her usual self. I stare down at my feet so I don't mindlessly gape at her as we wait for the crew to finish setting up the camera.

"God, it's so freakin' cold," Minjee hisses, bringing my attention back to her face. "Couldn't they tell us to stand on our marks *after* they finish setting up?"

I smile. Even though she may not look it, she's still the same Minjee I know.

"I know, right? They'd probably do that if we were more famous," I say. "Or if this show had a higher budget. I heard that for some shows, they get other people to stand in so the actors only have to come out when everything's ready."

"That'd be the absolute *dream*."

In a way, complaining about things behind the scenes with Minjee makes it feel like we're in school again, chatting backstage before we perform. It's the type of instant comradery that I've never had with anyone else.

A mischievous grin flashes across Minjee's face. "So, you're supposed to slap me today, right?"

"Um, yeah?" I say, taken aback by the change of topic.

"Well, don't hold back. Even if we're just doing fake slapping. I want it to be as realistic as possible. I won't even mind if you accidentally hit me. Let's try to get this scene done in as few takes as we can, okay?"

"Well, we *could* practice some slaps right now."

I glance back at the camera crew to see if anyone's watching. They're all crouched over the camera, talking about how they can't find a particular lens.

I turn back to Minjee with a playful grin of my own and add in English, "That is, unless you're too chicken."

Minjee scoffs. "Ever the American. Okay, I'm down. Let's try practicing."

Slapping someone on camera is always a tricky business because it requires a team effort between two actors. I feel a thrill at the challenge. Maybe this is my chance to follow through with my New Year's resolution and actually allow myself to have fun with this show.

I stand at an arm's length from her, positioning my feet wide enough that I have a stable stance. Minjee does the same, bracing herself.

"We should have a nonverbal cue," she says. "How about I blink to tell you that I'm ready, and you swing then?"

"Sure."

I wait for Minjee to blink, and then swing my arm. Minjee ducks well clear from my hand, so clear that it's definitely not going to look realistic, and especially not on camera.

We try a few more times, but they all look obviously fake.

"Maybe try a bit faster?" Minjee suggests.

"Okay."

She blinks. I swing. This time, my fingertips make contact with her cheek.

"Shoot!" I say. "Sorry."

Minjee only laughs. "Totally fine. Like I said, I don't care if you accidentally hit me. That was definitely more realistic, though, so try it again like that! I'll try to dodge faster."

This time, my fingers come so close to Minjee's cheek that I can feel her body heat, *without* making contact with her skin.

"Perfect! We've got this."

"Awesome!"

We high-five. We're both grinning ear to ear. Acting together feels so natural, like we're back in school practicing skits. When I'm with Minjee, it really isn't hard to have fun. I hope we can keep up this energy for the real thing.

"Okay, we're ready to go," says Director Cha. He must have seen us practice because he gives us an amused look. "Sorry for the wait. We thought we were ready, but there was something wrong with one of the lenses. The issue is fixed now."

When it's time to get into our places, I walk through the doorway of the main gates of the palace, which is where I'm supposed to enter through with my entourage of royal servants.

I bow to all the actresses who are playing my servants while we're waiting for the director to call action. They give me friendly waves in return. Even though they're my servants on-screen, they're all women around my mom's age. I want to treat them with the utmost respect.

"All right, action!" shouts Director Cha.

The ladies pick up the long skirts of my hanbok to help me walk up the steps and through the gate into the palace. We stride into the courtyard, and I keep my head held high as I survey my surroundings. My directions for this scene are simple yet spicy. Slap Danbi and tell her off for hanging out with Hyun. I've got this.

Feeling every bit like some mean girl in a high school drama show, I storm as quickly as I can in Minjee's direction. Minjee, as Danbi, takes a step back, a scared yet resolute look on her face.

But when I meet her eyes, Minjee winks. The camera's on me, so it won't capture her expression, and it takes all my effort not to smile. By the time I'm standing in front of her, though, Minjee's face is dead serious again, since her face might be visible in the periphery of the shot.

She greets me with her head bowed. I keep my nose pointed up to the sky. In this lifetime, Danbi is a maidservant while my character is a princess. I give her my best steely glare.

"My maidservants spotted you leaving the prince's chambers late at night. What could you possibly have had to do there?"

Minjee glares up at me, eyes flashing. Her gaze is so intense that it takes all my effort to not flinch away. As we're standing there, practically nose-to-nose, I linger on the little details on her face I wouldn't normally get to see unless I was this close up. Her mahogany-brown eyes. The light freckles across her cheeks.

I'm supposed to slap her after her next line. I get ready.

"The prince sought out my company," Minjee says. "I was there under his orders."

She blinks. I swipe my hand. She dodges perfectly, cutting it close enough that there are small gasps from the crew members.

"How dare you insinuate such things about the prince?" I yell. "I'm sure he had a good reason for asking you to be there. Repent before you find yourself kicked out of the palace."

I wish I could scrub my mouth with soap. I have no idea what direction the show was supposed to go in before they decided to add Minjee into the script, but I wish they hadn't made my character so . . . petty.

I turn around like I'm supposed to, and my entourage follows me across the courtyard. I don't totally leave the scene, though, because at that point Minjee comes in with, "With all due respect, agissi, you speak too harshly. And you struck out unfairly. We were just talking. Nothing more. Please ask the prince about what happened. If his words counter mine, I will gladly leave."

Chills go down my spine at the quiet resolve in Minjee's voice. The lines sounded so resigned when I read them in the script, but her tone gives them an edge that changes their meaning entirely.

I wish I had better lines to counter her. But my lines stop there. I'm just supposed to walk away as if I didn't hear her. And so, that's exactly what I do until Director Cha cries out,

"Cut! That was great, ladies. Reset! We'll be shooting from Sora's POV next."

On my way back to my mark, I stop to tell Minjee, "You were amazing."

"Thanks!" she replies. "You were good, too."

The compliment is nice, but it doesn't do much against how crummy I feel about the scene in general. Something in Minjee's expression tells me she feels the same way. I say quietly so only she can hear, "Thanks. I just wish I had better lines to work with."

Minjee's eyes widen. "Same!" she whispers back. "Wouldn't it be amazing if Sora and Danbi were secretly friends?"

"Or better yet, lovers?"

The question comes out of my mouth before I can stop it. Minjee laughs and says, "Oh gosh, that'd be so good! And then they could ride off into the sunset together while leaving Hyun in the dust."

"What are you two whispering about?" Director Cha asks, cutting our conversation short. "The camera is ready. Please get back to your places."

Minjee and I share one last secret grin before we return to our marks. Sora and Danbi being endgame is a scenario that'll probably never happen in a K-drama, but it's definitely fun to think about. And even though I'm sure Minjee was just playing along with what I said, it makes me feel better that she wasn't repulsed by the idea.

Before we begin again, Minjee says loud enough for everyone else to hear, "Take two. Hope you're ready, agissi. Because this time I'm going to be glaring even more daggers at you."

I throw a mock-victory sign in Minjee's direction. "Bring it. Because this princess isn't going down without a fight."

Everyone chuckles at our little exchange, and it takes me a lot of effort to stop smiling so we can run the scene again.

Chapter 18

WHEN I CHECK MY PHONE LATER THAT NIGHT, I
see a message from Minjee.

> **So, want to keep up a betting pool on who Hyun will end
> up with at the end of the drama?**

I don't know whether to be mad or amused. I text back:

what's the reward?

She replies almost immediately.

> **Hm, winner's pick?**

That could be anything. What if I ask you for a car?

> **LOL someone's confident!**

Minjee and I end up messaging each other for the next couple of days in between shoots and schoolwork. Soon enough, I
find myself waking up every morning looking forward to getting another text from her.

On set, though, we don't interact any more than we have to
besides the occasional smile or funny look. It's not something

we formally agreed on, but something about the secret nature of our friendship makes things more fun, especially when our characters are supposed to hate each other on the show.

I'm buried in my math coursework on my off day later that week, trying to wrap my head around various formulas when I get a message from Minjee.

Hey, wanna hang out later today?

I think back to how much fun Minjee and I had on Christmas and reply, **So totally down!** I'm about to press send when my thoughts flash back to what happened with Bryan on Namsan Tower.

This is different, I tell myself. *It's not like Minjee is going to tip off anyone that you two are hanging out. You've hung out with her before with no problem.*

After a few deep breaths, I manage to hit send. But I also add, **What do you have in mind?** I want to give myself the chance to say no if whatever Minjee suggests doesn't sit well with me.

Hm, how about Namdaemun Market at 10 PM? It's been a while since I've been there.

Namdaemun Market is the largest traditional market in Seoul. It has ten thousand vendors, and even more shoppers that come and go along the stalls. If there is anywhere in Seoul where Minjee and I can remain anonymous and discreet, this crowded and bustling market would be it.

Sure! Sounds good. See you then.

The thought of hanging out with Minjee again makes me happy. After my last disastrous social outing, I'm looking forward to hanging out with someone for fun and not as part of some elaborate scheme.

Or at least I tell myself that's why I'm buzzing with anticipation. Never mind that my entire day becomes instantly better whenever I get a text from Minjee. And I find myself smiling whenever I think of something she said.

This isn't the first time I've had a crush on another girl, but it's the first time I've felt this way about someone I actually know.

This is just another friend-date, I remind myself. *That's all!*

Even so, I still can't stop smiling as I continue working on my coursework. Not even mathematical equations are enough to sour my mood before I meet up with Minjee.

A few hours later, I'm waiting for Minjee at the exit for Hoehyeon Station, the subway station closest to Namdaemun Market. I'm bundled up in a parka and a scarf since it's freezing again. Only for a friend like Minjee would I even leave the apartment in this weather.

There's a tap on my shoulder, and I turn around to see Minjee standing next to me. She's similarly bundled up as well, except unlike my white coat and pink scarf, she's all gothic with a studded leather jacket and chic red Prada glasses that make her look stunning and fierce at the same time.

"Since when are you so edgy?" I ask with a laugh.

Minjee shrugs. "Just something I've been trying out lately. It's nice to be able to experiment with different clothes when we don't have to attend classes. Don't get me wrong, our school's sky-blue uniforms are better than most high schools'. But uniforms in general are so *soul-sucking* sometimes."

"Fair. I still remember how shocked I was when I first found out that all middle schoolers and high schoolers in Korea wear uniforms. Meanwhile, in the States, people wear all sorts of stuff to school."

Minjee dramatically sighs. "Maybe I was born in the wrong country."

I laugh. "Nah, there are still dress codes there. You'd probably get in trouble a lot."

Just the thought of Minjee wearing her current outfit to school makes me smile.

"Probably!" she admits with a goofy grin of her own.

We start walking toward the market.

"Is there anything you want to do in particular here?" I ask.

I've been to Namdaemun a few times with my mom, but we usually just shopped for last-minute groceries on our way back home. I have no idea what there is to do for fun here.

"I'm dying for some street food," Minjee replies. "Today is my cheat day. Remember how we used to stop by the vendors near school on our way home?"

I perk up. "Yeah! My mouth's watering just thinking about that really spicy hot dog we ate that one time."

"Yikes!" Minjee laughs. "Of course you'd still remember that. Personally, I blocked it out because of how bad it was."

I gasp, giving her an overly indignant look. "That's it. We can't be friends anymore."

"Kidding, kidding." Minjee gives my arm a good-natured tap. "But yeah, let's go look at the food stalls. I'm starving."

"Yes!"

We share an excited grin before walking into the market.

Even though it's past ten, the streets are bustling with people browsing through the stalls lit by bright lights. I still remember how shocked and overwhelmed I was when I first came here, since the hustle and bustle wasn't something I ever saw back in my quiet, sleepy town in Florida.

All around us, vendors sell everything from household appliances to pseudo designer bags and shoes. Small shops sell makeup, phone accessories, and everything else I can imagine, with marquee signs and TV screens playing advertisements on loop.

We pass by a skin-care ad with Minjee's face on it.

I point at it. Minjee grins.

"Yup, that's me!" She leans in and whispers in my ear, "My skin was good even before I used the product, though. But don't tell anyone that."

I gasp in mock horror. "I would have never guessed!"

Various K-pop songs play on the speakers of shops and

stalls. One of the most commonly played tracks is by NOVA, Bryan's boy band.

"No matter where we go, I can't escape him," I grumble.

Minjee lets out a surprised laugh and pats me on the back. "Trouble in paradise?"

That's when I remember that Minjee doesn't know Bryan's and my relationship isn't real. I want to tell her so badly, but I can't. I suppress an urge to groan.

"I guess you can say that," I say. "He's not exactly the K-pop prince dream-guy everyone thinks he is."

Minjee raises her eyebrows but doesn't pry further.

When we reach the food vendors, the aunties at the stalls hold out fresh, warm samples of steamed buns and fish cake in our general direction.

Minjee and I try out some of the food, but everything tastes so good that it's hard to decide what to spend our money on.

"I can't choose. I want to eat *everything*!" Minjee exclaims, looking truly overwhelmed.

"Okay, then, it's decided. We'll get one of everything," I quip.

We look at each other, and then start giggling. At this rate, we'll be stuck here forever.

"Let's just follow the crowd and see where the popular spots are?" suggests Minjee.

"Sure!"

She points at a group of kids around our age. Instead of stopping by different stalls like we were, they're making a bee-line for one specific destination.

"They look like they know what's good," Minjee says. "Let's see where they're headed."

We follow the group as they walk between the busy stalls. As we do, I hear bits and pieces of their conversation above the general din of the crowd.

"Ugh . . . it's so cold. I hate winter."

"Did you watch the latest episode of *Fated Destiny*?"

"Let's get some hot fish cake soup and tteokbokki."

Minjee and I exchange looks. It's probably not a good idea to follow this group if some of them have watched our show.

I'm about to suggest to Minjee that we should just pick a place ourselves when the group reaches a food vendor surrounded by a huge crowd of people. There are several other street food stalls around it, but the sitting area for this one is full of men in business suits drinking soju while feasting on spicy red tteokbokki and students holding juicy sticks of fish cakes while talking about random stuff. Its line is super long, too—a surefire sign that the place is really good.

As if that wasn't convincing enough, I hear people calling this place a "matjip," a place known to have yummy food.

"Okay, we *have to* eat here," I say, heading to the end of the line.

"Definitely," replies Minjee with a firm nod.

I smile. It's nice to know she's on the same page as me.

While we wait our turn to order, Minjee and I talk about anything and everything, from our favorite Korean dramas to our favorite street foods. We whisper so the people in front of us can't hear us and recognize our voices.

"No way, your favorite drama of all time is *Goblin*, too?" Minjee asks. "Weren't you living in the US back then?"

"Yeah, but plenty of people from the US watch Korean dramas. That's the entire reason why I got into acting in the first place!"

"Wow, I guess the power of Hallyu is real after all."

"Trust me, if it weren't for the Korean Wave, I'd still be back in Florida."

When we're at the front of the line, I clear my throat and order in a voice that's higher than my normal one. "One cup of tteokbokki and one stick of fish cake, please!"

Minjee gives me an amused grin. When it's her turn to order, she orders in a lower voice than normal. "I'll have the same. Thank you!"

I can barely suppress my urge to giggle.

"We should give each other fake names, too, while we're at it," Minjee says after we've gotten our food.

"Easy," I reply. "You can be Hanjee and I can be Mina. Our names remixed together."

Minjee laughs. "It's amazing how fast you came up with that."

I blush and pretend to be immensely preoccupied with my food to avoid meeting Minjee's eyes.

We don't talk much after that since the tteokbokki and fish cake from the shop turn out to be well worth the wait. I've had both countless times before, but the tteokbokki's sauce is just the right amount of spicy, while the rice cake has the perfect chewy texture. The fish cake's soup burns my throat on the way down, but it's salty and delicious, warming me up from head to toe. Together, the food practically melts in my mouth. It feels like coming home to a warm house on a cold winter day.

"Mmm, this is so good!" Minjee exclaims. Her glasses are all fogged up from the steam of the food, making her look somehow silly and adorable at the same time.

"Seriously! This is the best tteokbokki and fish cake I've had in my entire life!"

Neither of us says anything else until our bowls are empty. And it's only when I finish that I think to look around us. We're mostly surrounded by other kids around our age, although there are some older people in the shop as well.

"So, where to next, *Mina*?" Minjee asks.

"Do you have room for dessert? I think there's a good hotteok place a few stalls away from here."

"I always have room for dessert!"

Hotteok are my favorite kind of dessert. They're small pancakes filled with brown sugar, peanuts, honey, and cinnamon that melt in your mouth in a delicious, sugary way. The stall we go to sells them for cheap, so I buy two so I can give one to Minjee. The hotteok are nice and warm in my hands, which have started to get cold again from the frigid night air.

"You have pretty eyes!" the ahjumma taking my money says. "Are they real or did you get double eyelid surgery?"

The random, intrusive question would have been shocking to me when I first moved from the States, but today I just smile and answer with, "They're one hundred percent natural."

The ahjumma chuckles and turns away to tend to the next customer. Korean middle-aged women are so notorious for butting into everyone's business that after over four years of living in Korea, I'm used to interactions like this.

When I hand Minjee her hotteok, she holds it up in appreciation. "Thanks! Don't think this means I'll go easy on you in the show, though."

"I wouldn't expect anything less. Just buy me something the next time we get food."

"Definitely." She laughs and takes a bite out of the hotteok, her teeth sinking into the chewy, deep-fried bun with a satisfying crunch.

"Oh my God," she says between bites. Her breath fogs up in the cold night air as she says, "This is amazing."

I laugh. "I last had this hotteok a year ago and I've had dreams about it ever since."

"Well, thank you for introducing me to this heavenly food."

"You're welcome! I'm glad you like it."

While we eat our hotteok, we continue walking down the market street, browsing the stalls. We pass by everything from barking toy robot dogs to dried nuts for sale. The shops we pass this time *thankfully* aren't blasting music by NOVA and instead are playing trot, a type of loud and folksy-sounding pop music that a lot of old people listen to. Trot gets its name from its very distinct and sometimes laughably obnoxious fox-trot beat, and Minjee and I bounce up and down to the music.

Minjee giggles as she dramatically points left and right while swinging her hips. I laugh and join in. Soon we're both giggling and making complete fools of ourselves as we walk down the street.

While we dance, I realize this would have been the life Minjee and I could've had if we weren't actresses. We'd wander around these streets with our friends from school, eating street food and chatting as we tried to forget about impending final exams. I feel a bittersweet pang in my heart at the thought, a kind of longing that isn't a longing, not really, since it's not like I actually wish my life were like that.

I like my life the way it is now, even with its dramatic ups and downs. But I also can't deny that sometimes I wish it were a bit simpler. Then again, if I were a normal high school kid, I'd probably still be in the States right now, not in Korea.

I'm down to the last bite of my hotteok when I see the first flash. The bad thing about eating food is that we had to move our scarves down from our faces to do so. I thought it'd be fine since nothing happened at the food stall, but I was clearly wrong. The next thing I know, a few other people start taking pictures of us.

Minjee whispers, "They must have recognized us!"

All the peace I'd been feeling just moments before evaporates.

I look around for possible places to duck and hide, but I'm not familiar with this part of the market. There are just too many people around, and more and more of them turn around to whisper about us. It's only a matter of time before it becomes a full-blown crowd.

"Hey, I have an idea," Minjee says, her voice breaking through the haze of my panic. "Have you ever ridden a motorbike before?"

"Only for a show," I say. "And I wasn't driving it."

"Good enough."

Minjee grabs my arm, and we start running through the crowd.

"Park Minjee! Park Minjee!"

"Jin Hana!"

Shouts come from behind us. I glance back to see several people chasing us with their phones and cameras outstretched.

"Look where you're going!" Minjee shouts.

I turn back around just in time to narrowly avoid running into a kid.

The little boy bursts into tears. His mom shoots me an annoyed look.

"I'm so sorry!" I apologize as Minjee and I keep running.

We manage to lose most of the people chasing us. But it's only a matter of time before they'll catch up.

Minjee leads me to a dark back alley. For a split second, I question her judgment.

Then, we come across a sleek blue motorbike that looks

like it came straight out of an action movie.

"Whoa," I say. "Is this your bike? I thought you took the subway like I did."

"Nah," replies Minjee, taking the keys out from her jacket pocket. "I rode my bike. I just figured it'd be easier if we met at the stop. Here."

She tosses me a helmet. "Get on. Hold on tight so you don't fall off."

Minjee straddles the seat, and I get on behind her. Like she suggested, I wrap my arms around her, so we're awfully close, practically pressed against each other. But the most surprising part is how natural it feels. Minjee's body fits perfectly against mine.

"You ready?" Minjee asks, bringing me out of my thoughts. "Because they're gaining on us again."

I look behind us and see two guys running toward us in the alley. They're both carrying professional-grade cameras. Paparazzi.

"Yup," I say. "Let's go!"

Minjee presses down on the gas. The motorbike roars to life, shooting out of the alley and onto the road. I squeeze Minjee tightly, and if my vise grip bothers her, she doesn't say anything.

People spot us and yell at us again, but it doesn't matter. Adrenaline shoots down my spine as we whizz past them in a blink of an eye. I feel so free, like how I felt while riding the roller coaster. By the time Minjee's bike joins the busy Seoul traffic, we've completely lost our pursuers.

"That was amazing!" I shout as Minjee's bike weaves through cars. "Where did you learn how to drive a motorbike like that?"

"A crappy ex-boyfriend," Minjee replies with a giggle. "He was a bad kisser, but at least he was useful for something!"

We laugh, and as we continue riding below the sparkling city lights, I realize I can't keep ignoring how I really feel about Minjee.

Chapter 19

IT'S STILL DARK OUTSIDE WHEN SOPHIA PICKS ME up at my apartment the next morning. Normally I can go to all the shooting locations myself using public transportation, but today we're shooting at a beach in Gangwon-do, which is almost three hours away on the other side of the country.

"Hey," I say when I get in the car. "Thank you so much for taking me to the beach."

"No problem," she replies. "I still don't know why they couldn't just film around Seoul, but I guess it's nice to leave the city for a bit."

Gangwon-do is my favorite province in Korea because it has beautiful mountains and stunning beaches. It's basically where everyone goes camping or skiing, depending on the season. A lot of K-dramas film iconic moments there every year since the scenery is so stunning.

I feel bad that Sophia has to drive me so far, but I'm really excited to get out of the city.

"So," Sophia says once we're on the highway, "I saw the news about you and Minjee. Well done! That'll catch people's attention for sure. I'm actually disappointed in myself for not being the one to come up with the idea of you and her being friends."

Since yesterday, stories about Minjee and me ended up everywhere online. Compared to how scandalous the headlines about Bryan and me were, these ones are pretty innocuous, talking about how ironic and cute it is that we're close enough friends to hang out off set when we're supposed to be mortal enemies on-screen.

I smile. After much debate, I'd decided not to tell Sophia that I'm hanging out with Minjee. Nor did I tell her that I know Minjee from school. I wasn't sure how she'd react to the idea of us being friends, but now I'm relieved she seems on board with the whole thing.

"Thanks," I reply. "I'm glad everyone reacted so positively to the news."

Even though there's probably no harm in Sophia knowing about Minjee and me, I wanted to keep our friendship a secret, even from her. Everything I do nowadays is so public, ending up in news headlines all over the world. I want to keep my friendship with—and these new feelings for—Minjee as close to my heart as I can.

When we arrive, I'm relieved to see that the beach is pretty much empty, thanks to the cold temperatures and gray skies. What I'm *not* glad to see is that everyone is weirdly nicer to me than usual. Bryan's assistant even smiles at me and asks if I "want water or anything." Before I can say no, he shoves a boxed water into my hand.

Darn it! I stare at the box of water in dismay. The one old Batman movie quote about living long enough to see yourself become the villain flashes in my mind.

I'm incredibly thirsty after the long drive, though, so I begrudgingly end up opening up the carton anyway. While I'm drinking, I realize what's going on. Today's my first time on set with Bryan since our official relationship announcement.

The assistant cups her face with one hand and whispers, "He's here!" to me, smiling like we share a secret.

I manage to give her a tight grin in response.

And sure enough, Bryan strides onto set, dressed in a sleek black stealth suit. According to the call sheet, he has a lot of action scenes to film today, since we're almost at the big climax of the show.

"Hey," he says to me. "How've you been?"

"Hi," I reply. "I've been okay. How about you?"

"Oh, cool. I've been all right."

His expression is guarded, and it takes me a moment to understand why. While he talks over scene directions with Director Cha, I pull out my phone from my pocket.

4 unread messages from Bryan Yoon

I'd been having so much fun talking and hanging out with Minjee throughout the week that I completely forgot that Bryan texted me. *Oops.*

I open up the conversation.

hey, so . . . wanna talk about what happened at the tower?

hello

sorry are you mad

ok talk to you later

I'm trying to figure out what I can say to him when Director Cha says, "All right, let's get started, everyone!"

Bryan and I have a few lines together before he has to do his action scenes. Despite the awkwardness between us, we're not noticeably bad, and we still play off each other well. The takes we film must be satisfactory because Director Cha doesn't yell "Cut!" more often than he usually does. There's an unmistakable tenseness in Bryan's eyes, and it doesn't go away when the camera stops rolling. Luckily, the scenes we're shooting are pretty edgy anyway, which fits the gloomy beach we're at well.

When I'm done for today, I check the time. We're thankfully running ahead of schedule for once. I take a deep breath and walk over to where Bryan is discussing action scenes with the stunt coordinator, a big, muscular man in his forties.

"Hi, um, excuse me," I say.

The stunt coordinator harrumphs. I bow at him before I continue. "Could I please speak to Bryan for a sec? It won't be long, I promise."

I don't do my own stunts like Bryan does—something I really hope to change one day—so I've never really had to interact with the stunt coordinator much. Something about his really thick arm muscles and squarish jaw makes him really intimidating.

The two guys exchange glances before Bryan grins at him apologetically.

"Agh, who am I to keep two young love birds apart?" the stunt coordinator finally shouts, his booming voice making me jump. "Make it quick! Just because we're ahead of schedule today doesn't mean you can dillydally for long."

"Thank you, sir." Bryan gives him a big bow before raising his eyebrows at me.

"Come on," I say. "Let's talk somewhere more private."

We head down to the beach, which is a few yards away from the rocky overlook where the crew's set up the camera. It's freezing, and the spray of the seawater is icy cold, but something about the rolling expanse of the waves makes me feel at peace.

When I turn back to look at Bryan, I can't help but notice how the wind is tousling his wavy hair, which, coupled with the stormy look in his eyes, makes him the perfect K-drama hero. For countless other girls, being liked by someone like Bryan is probably a dream come true. But not me. I *am* excited and proud to see how amazing he'll look on-screen, though.

"So," I say. "First, I'm sorry for being MIA this week. I got caught up in a lot of things. But I also wanted to tell you that nothing's changed from the last time we talked." I pause, wondering how I can drive things home this time without giving

Bryan any false hope. It's probably best to tell him the truth. Or at least part of it. "I don't like you in that way. I . . . actually like someone else."

The moment I say it, it occurs to me that I might have said too much.

Bryan immediately jerks to attention. "Who?"

If we were in a less conservative society, I would have just told him the truth right then and there. But since we're in Korea, and I have no idea how Bryan feels about queer people like me, I just say, "I want to keep that a secret, at least for now. Enough of our private lives are leaked constantly already."

Bryan sighs. "Fair."

He turns around to leave. I'm about to relax my guard when he abruptly whips back toward me. "Wait . . . is it Minjee?"

It takes everything in my power to not react, to keep totally calm as I stare at Bryan point-blank. He doesn't *look* like he's repulsed by the idea of me liking Minjee, but there's no way to tell how he really feels. We're both actors. If I can hide my true thoughts and feelings, so can he.

The ocean's roar grows deafening. I clench my fists, gathering up all my strength so I don't run away.

Bryan continues, "I mean, come on. It's pretty obvious. You and I have both been busy with the show for the last few months. And I imagine you have a lot of schoolwork to do off set like I do. It's unlikely you've had much time to hang out with anyone else. I've also seen all the pictures from when you've hung out with Minjee. You look way happier in them than you did whenever we hung out. It's either Minjee or some random internet stranger, I'm calling it."

If I weren't so terrified at the fact that Bryan guessed correctly, I'd laugh at "random internet stranger." I stare at him, trying to decide if I trust him. I think back to the moment we shared in the cable car, at how honest he'd been about his own feelings with me in the past. Sure, he's ridiculous sometimes, but he hasn't done anything that makes me think he's a bad person. Maybe I *can* trust him after all.

"Please don't tell anyone," I finally say. "I don't even know if Minjee likes me back. If anyone finds out about my feelings for her, it'd—"

"Ruin your entire career, I know," he cuts in, looking out across the sea.

I flinch. My heart's racing so fast that it feels like it's about to burst when he says, "Isn't it funny and sad how people just assume everyone is straight? Like why is that the default, especially in Korea?"

He still has his back turned toward me, so I know his question is probably rhetorical. But this is something I've asked myself a lot, too. "Because being queer means you're different," I answer. "It means you don't fit in with the traditional gender roles that are prevalent in Korean society. And some people are also against it for religious reasons."

"Right. I guess wherever we go there will be people opposed to it. But isn't it wild how, on the other side of the Pacific,

174

there are people like us that can marry their same-sex partners and have laws that protect them? I think about it a lot. Not so much the marrying part, but the other stuff."

"Wait," I say, reeling from whiplash. "'People like us'?"

Bryan runs a hand through his hair, finally turning around to give me his dazzling K-pop prince smile. "I'm pan. Or at least I'm questioning. I didn't know what that was until I saw some stuff about it on Twitter. But everything more or less made sense after that. I've had this lifelong crush on one of my family friends. He's bi, but he's dating a girl he met in LA and they're happy together, so, eh."

He shrugs, and his smile fades into a wry grin.

"Wow" is all I can say. I drop down to a crouch, falling into what can only be described as a contemplative ahjumma sitting pose, since it's how a lot of Korean aunties at the market sit while they sell their crops.

"Is me being pan that surprising?" Bryan laughs. "Well, at least now you know you have nothing to be worried about. Your secret is safe with me. As long as . . . you know—"

I shoot back up to a standing position and nod. "Of course, I'll definitely keep your secret safe, too."

We stand side by side in companionable silence, looking out at the sea for a long moment before I ask, "Do you know anyone else like us in the industry? I mean, of course I've heard of Holland and a handful of other queer adults. But anyone closer to our age?"

I can't keep the hope out of my voice.

"Yeah! The guy I had a crush on is a model. And his girl-friend is a K-pop star. I'm telling you . . . queer people . . . we're everywhere! The industry—this *country!*—just doesn't know it yet."

"We should honestly plan a queer takeover. Just paint rain-bows all over Sangam-dong."

"Hah! The world's not ready for when we're old enough to go clubbing at Itaewon."

I laugh along with Bryan, but the mention of clubs makes me a bit nervous. A few years ago, a lot of people in South Korea were quick to demonize the queer community because some outbreaks during a pandemic were traced to gay clubs in Seoul. I hope things will be better by the time Bryan and I are old enough to go out.

"But yeah," Bryan says, "the fact that you don't like me because you like a girl makes me feel a lot better. Definitely a lot easier on my ego."

I raise an eyebrow at Bryan. "Excuse you. I like both guys and girls, just not *you*. So that's very faulty logic on your part. Plus, your ego doesn't need any help."

He grins. "True, true."

"Bryan! Hana!" Director Cha yells at us. He's power walk-ing across the beach toward us from where the crew's set up. The sand's sticking to his pants, and he looks miserable. "What are you two doing? Bryan, we need to shoot the next scene!"

"My cue to leave," Bryan says with a wink. "But good talk,

Jin! And best of luck with the whole unrequited crush thing!"

Jin? I'm still processing the fact that he called me by my last name when Bryan breaks off into a run, bowing and enthusiastically apologizing to the director.

What a weird guy, I think. But despite the whirlwind of our conversation, I'm glad it happened. I feel really relieved that there are other queer kids like me in the industry.

I look back out at the water again, enjoying one last whiff of the salty air before I head back to where Sophia's waiting for me on set.

Now I just have to figure out what I'm going to do about Minjee.

Chapter 20

THE NEXT DAY, I'M WORKING ON SOME SCHOOL-work when I get a call from Director Cha.

I do a double take when I see his name on my phone screen. I'd saved his number at the very beginning of shooting, but I never expected him to ever call me himself. Usually he gets an assistant director or a production assistant to contact us.

"Um, hello?" I brace myself.

"Hana-ssi? Hello, this is Director Cha," he says. Compared to how informally he addresses us on set, I'm surprised by how polite he's being now. Something must be really wrong.

"Yes, this is she," I reply. "Is everything okay?"

Director Cha lets out a short sigh. "Okay, I'm going to cut to the chase. There was a slight problem with the editing on episode twelve, the one that will air tonight."

"Problem? What sort of problem?"

"Remember how we became delayed right after Miss Park joined us? Fortunately, we were able to catch up fairly quickly, thanks to everyone's hard work."

Boy, do I remember. "Yes, I do. Is there something that needs to be re-shot?"

"No, no, nothing like that. The error is very slight, not worth reshooting. But it has to do with your Korean, which is why I'm giving you this call."

"My Korean?"

I break into a cold sweat, and my palms feel clammy. Usually if my Korean sounds weird, someone from either the cast or crew points it out for me since everyone knows that Korean is my second language. No one has said anything so far. I'd assumed I was doing fine.

"There is this one moment in the dialogue with you and Minjee where your Korean sounds a bit . . . awkward. We tried to not use that take, but unfortunately, due to our rush to get back on track, we weren't able to find a better one to replace it. I assure you it's the best one in terms of your acting skills, however."

My stomach feels like it's dropped down to my feet. Sounding awkward on a television show with millions of viewers around the world is one of my worst nightmares. I'd just gotten over my fears of being an imposter, too.

"I apologize," Director Cha continues. "Normally, we'd catch the error in time, but you have to understand, these little accidents happen on shows. We're lucky that no one's left a Starbucks cup lying around like they did on *Game of Thrones*, and we're on a tighter schedule than they were!"

The joke is obviously meant to make me laugh, so I politely do, even though I have no idea what he's talking about. I was five when *Game of Thrones* first came out and never got around to watching it. I've never been as big on American TV shows as I am with K-dramas.

"But yes," the director finally says, "the ADs and I will be more attentive next time so something like this doesn't happen again."

"Thanks for letting me know."

After he hangs up, I call Sophia. She doesn't pick up, but when I text her what's wrong, she replies, **Stay off social media for a bit and it'll blow over. In the grand scheme of things, it's just one line. Chances are, most people won't notice, and the ones who decide to put you on blast for it aren't people you want as your fans anyway. It's not like it's a secret that you were born in the States. Only petty or rude people would make a big deal out of it.**

It's solid advice, so I exhale a bit to try to calm myself down. It's only a few hours before the episode airs. I might as well accept my fate.

The backlash thankfully isn't as bad as I thought it would be, but it's still brutal. Although most people are understanding of my Korean since I'm a "jaemi gyopo"—a Korean American—others aren't so nice. Some even make memes out of my mispronunciation, while others question how I ended up getting cast for the role in the first place. They ask why I, an American, was cast for this lead role when there are plenty of "actually Korean" stars out there who can do a better job.

After the episode ends, I get into bed early and read everyone's comments online, my eyes prickling with tears. Even though I love acting and enjoy being a part of *Fated Destiny*, I feel more like an imposter than I've ever felt. Mom and Dad come into my room to check in on me after they get off work, but I tell them I want to be left alone.

Several hours of scrolling later, I'm about to finally try to get some sleep when I get a message from Minjee.

Hey, I heard about what happened. How are you holding up?

I'm too tired to even put my thoughts into words, so I just send her back three crying emojis. She responds with a sad face, and suddenly she's calling me.

I reject her video chat request and call her back using audio only.

"Sorry," I say quietly. My voice sounds so defeated even to my own ears. "I'm lying in my bed in the dark, so you wouldn't have been able to see my face."

"Aw, that's okay," Minjee replies. I hear shifting noises as she moves around before she continues, "For what it's worth, I don't think you're not fit for this role. Sure, you weren't born here, but that doesn't mean you're not Korean. You're here now! Trying your best like the rest of us. And you're a super-talented actress, too! Heck, you beat me for this role! How dare they say you can't act? Haters just love to hate, honestly."

"Thanks for saying that." I've started to cry again, and I try my best not to let her hear me sniffle.

I must not have been successful, because Minjee's voice is noticeably softer and gentler when she continues, "Hey, I have an idea. Meet me at Gwanghwamun Square tomorrow at three in front of the King Sejong statue. Let's have some fun."

I'm pretty confused by what Minjee's saying, but I'm far too exhausted to question her.

"Okay," I say.

"Cool. See you then!"

I end the call, wondering what in the world I've signed myself up for.

Chapter 21

I GET TO THE STATUE OF KING SEJONG THE GREAT a few minutes early. Minjee isn't here yet, so I peer up at the bronze statue of the famous monarch who invented the Korean alphabet with a trusted team of scholars in the 1400s. It's a massive statue, majestic and shiny in the middle of the busy and bustling urban square. As I stare at its outstretched hand and regal throne, I can't help but wonder what King Sejong would think of me, a Korean girl who was born a whole ocean and continent away and had to painstakingly learn—and still sometimes struggles with—the language he invented.

I hope he'd be proud of me. At least I'm trying, right?

"Hey!" Minjee says as she reaches me. "Glad you could make it. I have a whole day planned for us. Are you okay with a bit of walking?"

Instead of her usual full face of dramatic makeup, Minjee has on her more natural look, which is how the hair and makeup ladies do her makeup when we're on set. She's gorgeous either way, but her more plain makeup confuses me since we're not shooting any scenes today.

"Yeah, that's fine! But where are you taking me?" I ask, equal parts amused and wary.

"You'll see," she just says with a wink.

We head up north toward the Gyeongbokgung Royal Palace gates, where majestic hanbok-clad palace guards stand at attention with their flags and spears. At first, I think we're going into the palace grounds, but Minjee leads me around the gates to a street with lots of shops.

As we're walking, we're surrounded by people from all over the world, dressed in both modern and traditional Korean clothes alike, eating street food and speaking in different languages. Wherever I look, I see groups taking selfies together in their rented-out hanbok, or just browsing the stalls and gift shops. I've never been to this part of the city before—my parents and I just went directly to the palace or the museums around it—so I'm fascinated . . . and I'm pretty sure I know what Minjee has in store for me.

"Are we here to rent hanbok?" I ask after we pass by a storefront window with a mannequin in a beautiful bright red hanbok.

Minjee grins. "That's the first part, yeah."

The last and one of the only times I wore a hanbok was for *Fated Destiny*, so I have no idea how today will go. But I still let Minjee lead me into one of the cute hanbok shops. The store is pretty crowded inside, filled with both Koreans and non-Koreans alike. Racks of many different hanbok pieces from blouses to skirts to accessories like hats and fake flowers line the walls of the store, with busy employees bustling about to direct people to the changing stalls.

One of the employees, a lady who looks around my mom's age, glances at us and does a double take.

"Jin Hana and Park Minjee?" she says with a gasp. "From *Fated Destiny?*"

In that instant, dozens of people snap their attention to us, pulling out their phones or whispering excitedly among themselves. I smile and give everyone mini bows while Minjee bows at the lady and replies, "Yes, that's us. We'd like to rent two hanbok, please. For us to try on for fun, not for the show."

The lady shakes our hands. When she pulls away, I see that she's left her business card in mine. I have to smile at her business savvy.

"Of course, of course," she says. "Welcome! I'm the manager of this store. Let me show you our most beautiful collection. And just so you know, whatever you rent today is totally on us. Please do put in a good word for us to the people at the studio, though."

"Will do!" replies Minjee. "Thank you."

The lady leads us past the crowded general room to a secluded room with a smaller but definitely more luxurious selection of hanbok. These look so delicate with their fine golden embroidery and pastel colors. With just one glance, I can tell they're way more expensive than the ones in the main room. My jaw drops at how beautiful they are.

"We couldn't possibly rent these for free," I protest before the lady leaves. "Please, let us pay you!"

She shakes her head furiously like I've insulted her. "Nonsense! You will do no such thing. Please just walk around the city and take lots of photos. I can guarantee that alone will bring us a lot of profit."

I still feel bad about the whole thing, but the lady looks so determined that I just bow at her again. "Okay, thank you."

"Take as long as you'd like to choose!" she says before closing the door behind her.

"Hey, Hana!" Minjee exclaims. "Come here for a sec!"

I turn around to see Minjee holding out a gorgeous hanbok with a pearl-white blouse and a pink skirt with elegant flowers embroidered on it. The skirt has a golden hem as a nice finishing touch and the blouse has a pink bow. It's gorgeous yet understated. Beautiful yet airy. The more I look at it, the more I notice intricate details in the design.

"This hanbok was made for you," she says. "You should try it on! I found a matching one for me, too."

In her other hand, she holds up a hanbok that's similar to mine but has a bright red skirt instead of a pastel pink one.

"I can't wait to see how cute we'll look in these." Minjee gives me a wide, toothy grin, and I can't help it. I smile back. Her enthusiasm is contagious.

We help each other into our hanbok, and when we're done, our reflections in the mirror make me grin so wide that my face hurts. The hanbok in *Fated Destiny* are gorgeous, but they're super formal—to be as historically accurate as possible—and honestly sometimes even suffocating. They make both Minjee and me look older than we really are. Now, though, we look like two normal high school girls in pretty but elegant hanbok.

Minjee and I snap as many selfies together as possible. As we're throwing up victory signs and making faces at the camera, I feel really giddy.

A sense of déjà vu washes over me, and I ask Minjee, "Do you remember that time we went to take pictures at the photo booth? Before we even read the scripts for *Fated Destiny*?"

Minjee's eyes light up in recognition. "Yeah, of course! I still have one of the photos saved as my KakaoTalk profile pic, I think."

"Yeah, you do. To be honest, I looked at that photo a lot when I first started *Fated Destiny*. I think I was just really lonely since I wasn't going to school and everything. But I was afraid to reach out to you because I felt bad about getting the lead part when you didn't."

Minjee frowns and places a hand on my shoulder. "Hana . . ."

I look into her warm brown eyes. I can't even come close to expressing how much she means to me, how I'm so scared of telling her how I really feel because I don't want to lose the friendship we have.

So I just say, "Thanks for reaching out when you did. It helped a lot."

She gives my shoulder a gentle squeeze. "No problem."

We stand there for a moment, smiling at each other. There's a palpable tension buzzing between us, like we're about to kiss. But then Minjee looks away. It's probably just my wishful thinking.

"Okay! Let's get moving. This is only phase one. We have two more phases to go!"

I laugh. Her enthusiasm is so adorable. "Okay, where to next?"

We leave the hanbok store, but not before being greeted by a sea of fans that crowds the main room. I catch sight of the manager lady looking on with pride and approval as we take selfies with fans.

"We have the hanbok for four hours . . . which is more than enough time for what we're going to do today," Minjee says when we leave the store. "That is, provided that we don't get stopped at every block. Hopefully we won't."

Luckily, once we're out of the store, people pretty much leave us alone as we walk down the street. And I don't blame them. Minjee has a determined look on her face, like she's on a mission and can't be disturbed. It probably looks intimidating to people who don't know her that well, but to me she looks really cute.

We end up retracing our steps back to Gyeongbokgung again, walking around the white-brick palace walls and crossing the street to follow a twisting and turning narrow path past little shops and restaurants. People smile at us as we walk by, surreptitiously and sometimes even overtly taking pictures of Minjee and me.

Minjee and I pick up rice cake waffles and black sesame lattes from a café so we can snack as we browse the shops we encounter along the way. Most of the stores are clearly targeted for tourists and sell things like traditionally designed pencil cases and Korean flag fans. But I enjoy browsing through everything all the same.

"Okay, almost there," Minjee says about an hour later.

When we turn the corner, we're suddenly surrounded by the traditional houses of Bukchon Hanok Village. Snow covers the black giwa tiles of the roofs, which, along with the wooden doors and window frames of the houses, make it seem like we've been transported back in time to Korea in the long-distant past. The only things that break the illusion are the streetlights and tourists taking photos with their smartphones. Some passersby are dressed in hanbok like we are, but others are in modern-day coats and jackets.

In retrospect, I should have guessed that this was where Minjee was taking me, but I gape in wonder all the same. I take a few quick pictures, marveling at the finely preserved antique quality of the houses.

Minjee leads me up the hilly street, all the while explaining to me that these houses still have people living in them.

"Even though it's a popular tourist attraction, it's a residential area, so we have to speak quietly so we don't disturb anyone."

I look around the houses, amazed at the idea that modern-day families actually live in these beautiful traditional homes. "Can you imagine just casually owning one of these houses? How cool would that be?"

"I know, right? Apparently, they're pretty expensive, though. And cost a lot to maintain."

Minjee and I continue walking up the hill, pausing here and there to take selfies with the pretty houses. When we reach the top of the hill, Minjee holds out her hand.

"Here," she says. "Let me take pictures of you. Glam photo shoot time! Stand over there."

She points at the middle of the street, where a lot of other people are pausing to take pictures, too. It doesn't take long for me to realize why—from where we're standing on the hill, there's a gorgeous view of the Seoul city skyline below. I wait for a group to finish taking pictures before standing at the spot where Minjee pointed.

"Smile!" she says. "Say kimchi!"

At that, my lips spread into a genuine smile. Unlike in the US, where people say "cheese," people in Korea say "kimchi" . . . which is probably the most Korean thing ever. It never fails to make me laugh whenever someone says it.

"Beautiful! Fabulous!" Minjee shouts. She crouches down—which looks really comical with her poufy hanbok skirt—and flips my phone at different angles, taking multiple shots like she's some professional photographer. "Fantastic! Stunning!"

I end up bent over, giggling at how ridiculous she's being.

"Okay," Minjee says when she's done. "Come look!"

To avoid walking into a passing group of people, I jog around as quickly as I can in the hanbok to where Minjee is. She hands me my phone, which has a picture of me pulled up on it.

"Swipe through these photos and tell me that this girl doesn't belong in Korea," Minjee says. "I dare you."

I do what she says, and I'm shocked by how beautiful the pictures look. The scenery is pretty enough in person, but the phone camera adds a focused quality that makes the contrast between the traditional houses and urban skyline look stunning. And then there's me, standing in the middle of all that. Minjee snapped photos all the way up until she told me to come look, so I can see the progression from me smiling to me breaking into hysterical laughter. I look so happy, and most importantly, Minjee is right. I do look like I belong in this city, with its complex and eclectic mix of the old and the new.

I flip back to the pictures Minjee and I took together today around the city.

Before I know it, I'm sniffling. Tears are falling fast.

I feel a gentle grasp on my wrist and look up to see Minjee's worried expression.

"Whoa there," she says. "You okay?"

"Yeah," I tell her, pausing to wipe my tears away. "Sorry. Today has just been so good. I'm grateful to have you in my life."

"Aw, Hana." Minjee's eyes get shiny, like she's about to tear up, too, before she rapidly shakes her head. "But wait! We're not done yet! There's one last phase left."

I burst into surprised laughter, definitely no longer crying. "Okay, let's go!"

Minjee holds out her hand. It takes me a moment to remember that in Korea, it's perfectly normal for girls to hold hands when walking around. I slowly put my hand in hers, and my heart pounds in my chest as we walk the rest of the way up the hill together.

We pass by the houses and reach a broader street. I'm about to ask where we're headed when Minjee stops and says, "Look!"

I glance at where she's pointing and am once again amazed by the sight in front of me. While just moments before, we could see the city from where we were standing, we now have a picturesque view of Gyeongbokgung's tallest buildings. The Royal Palace looks stately from where we're standing. Complete with the surrounding mountains and the golden rays of the slowly setting sun in the horizon, it's a sight fit for a Korean drama.

"Wow," I say. "This is amazing. Minjee, I honestly don't know how many times I can thank you. You're such an incredible friend and I . . ."

I glance away from the view and trail off when I notice Minjee's staring at me with a weird look in her eyes. Even though I've known her for years, I can't place the expression on her face. Before I can figure out what it is, she drops her gaze to our joined hands and gives mine a slight squeeze.

"Glad you like it," she says. Compared to how loud and enthusiastic she was being before, her sudden, quiet solemnness has me worried.

Did I do something wrong? I wonder. But no matter how hard I try, I can't think of what might have upset her.

"Minjee?" I ask. "Is everything okay?"

She lets go of my hand and gets out her phone. "Of course! Now get up on that step by that fence. I want to take pictures of you with this view before the sun completely sets."

I do as she says, and she snaps a few pictures.

Then, with a quick "Let's go back before it gets dark," she turns and walks away.

Chapter 22

MINJEE DOESN'T RESPOND TO ANY OF MY TEXTS, not even when I send her the photos we took together. She just leaves me on read, message after message.

Maybe she just got busy, I tell myself. But there's a part of me that knows that something is wrong, especially after the look on her face the last time I saw her.

On Tuesday, I send her a text saying, **Hey, are you okay?** No response. Just read. We don't have any scenes together this week, so I have no excuse to see her in person. But Bryan does, so at the end of our shooting day, I ask him, "Hey, do you know if Minjee is okay?"

Bryan cocks his head to the side. "Huh? Yeah, I filmed a scene with her yesterday. She seemed fine, as far as I could tell. Didn't you guys hang out on Sunday?"

"Yeah. But she was acting kind of weird, or at least she was at the end of the day. I think something happened, but I have no idea what. We didn't fight or anything."

"Want me to ask her what's wrong? I have a stunt training session with her at the dojang on Friday."

"Dojang?" I ask. The only meaning for "dojang" I know is "stamp," but that's probably not what he means.

Bryan laughs. "Oh, sorry. I think Americans just call it a dojo, but in Korean it's dojang. Like a dojo, but it's for tae-kwondo, not karate."

"Ah." My cheeks redden. You'd think that after several years of living in Korea, I'd stop encountering new words, but nope.

Bryan's expression softens. He gives me an encouraging fist bump on my shoulder.

"It's okay," he says. "There's no way you could have known that unless you did martial arts. Maybe this is a sign that you should do your own stunts."

"Ugh, I would if Director Cha gave me some . . . but no, crown princesses like me just have to sit still, look pretty, and get rescued."

"I mean, but are you really complaining about getting rescued by a hot prince like me, though?"

I give Bryan a searing look. "Yes, Bryan. I am. A lot."

He laughs. Some things never change.

"Okay, okay," Bryan finally says. "But yeah, I can ask her if you want."

"Nah, it's okay. It feels kind of weird for my fake boyfriend to talk to the girl I have a crush on for me. Thanks, though."

Bryan wrinkles his nose. "Yeah, if you put it that way, that does sound awkward. Well, good luck! Let me know if there's any way I can help."

The only bright spot of my entire week is Wednesday evening, when Director Cha gathers everyone on set around for a special announcement.

"I'm happy to inform you all that the studio has decided to extend *Fated Destiny* for four more episodes!" he says, looking very pleased with himself. "The show's popularity is only getting better thanks to all of your hard work. Congratulations."

We all cheer. Everyone is in a really good mood after that, although there's also an undercurrent of anxiety. K-dramas are usually sixteen episodes long but are extended for a few more episodes if the show is really popular . . . whether or not the plot can be stretched out that long. This week, we were beginning to shoot what we thought were the last three episodes. But now, there are four more. It'll be interesting to see what the creative team comes up with next.

On my way home that night, I call Minjee. I miss being able to talk to her about what's going on in the show and want to check on her to make sure she really is okay. Since she left my messages on read the last few times I tried to reach her, though, I don't expect her to pick up.

But she does. Or at least I think she does. The ringing stops, but I hear nothing on the other line.

"Hello?" I say. "Minjee?"

"Hi, Hana." Minjee's voice sounds really stiff like it did the last time we talked. "Can I help you?"

Her really formal question throws me off. She's talking to me like she's a customer service representative and not my friend.

"Um, Minjee, are you okay?" I ask. "Look, if I did something wrong . . . please tell me. Whatever it is, I'm sorry."

Minjee lets out a deep sigh. "You didn't do anything wrong, Hana. I just . . ." She trails off, and for a long moment, she doesn't say anything.

"You just?"

She takes a sharp breath. "I can't be friends with you anymore. I know that sounds really mean, but it's not your fault and it's complicated. So please stop texting or calling me, okay?"

"Wait, what—"

Minjee hangs up, cutting me off. *What the—?*

I bring my feet up to where I'm sitting in the bus, wrap my hands around my knees, and watch the world outside go by as I try to make sense of what just happened.

The next day, I'm a total mess. I forget my lines and I come in when it's not my cue. It gets so bad that Director Cha yells at me, "Leave and come back when you're ready to take this more seriously!"

I bow apologetically and walk away from where the crew's set up.

We're shooting scenes at the Starfield Library in the COEX Mall at Gangnam today, which means all the people standing by the barriers we've set up to prevent disruptions saw me getting scolded by the director. And probably took pictures of it.

I pull up the hood of my jacket over my face and sit alone at one of the tables. On-location scenes at public places like this are sometimes fun but also nerve-racking. Thankfully, people are usually respectfully quiet when the camera is rolling, but it sucks to have a live audience watching every bad take you do.

From where I'm sitting, I stare up at one of the huge, two-storied floor-to-ceiling bookcases of the library. Golden-white lights line the shelves, creating a luminous and calming effect. Since I don't want to think about anything else, I scan the books on the shelves, trying to see if I've read any of them.

"Hey!"

I look up to see Bryan running toward me, accompanied by the enthusiastic hoots and cheers of our onlookers.

"Are you okay?" he asks after flashing everyone a bright grin.

I beckon him over.

He sits down across from me at the table and whispers so only I can hear, "Okay, what's up?"

"It's Minjee," I say. "I finally got a hold of her yesterday and she said she suddenly doesn't want to be friends with me anymore. I've known her since middle school! And as far as I know, nothing's happened between us, so . . . I'm really confused."

Bryan sits back in his chair and crosses one leg on top of the other, winking back at the crowd when they scream at his pose.

I groan. "I really can't have a conversation with you like this."

"Sorry," Bryan says, not sounding at all apologetic. "But, okay. She didn't give you any reason at all when you spoke to her? Not even a 'Wow, Hana, you're such a jerk!'?"

I laugh when Bryan tries to imitate Minjee. He overshoots his voice, so he ends up sounding more like a chipmunk than an actual human being.

"Funny, but no," I reply.

Bryan frowns but doesn't say anything.

"What?" I ask.

He sighs. "Okay. It's probably not my place to interfere, but I *really* want to finish today's scenes so we can get out of here. And it'd suck for production to be delayed again. So . . ."

"So?"

"What if I gave you a chance to talk to her again, but face-to-face this time? Remember how I said I'm going to be at the dojang with her tomorrow? You *could* come by and talk to her then, after we're finished training, that is. Want the address?"

Some part of me wonders if talking to Minjee face-to-face will even change anything. But I want to do anything I can to save my friendship with her.

"If it isn't too much trouble," I say. "That'd be great."

"Okay, I'll text you. But can you *please* brush up on your

lines real quick and focus so we can go home already?"

I nod. "Thanks, and yeah, will do. Give me a few minutes and I'll be ready to go."

"Thank you *very* much," Bryan dramatically says in English. "Let's finish up."

Energized by the hope of being able to talk to Minjee, I quickly go over my lines and rejoin everyone else. We finish the scenes in half the time we—okay, I—spent making mistakes.

Later that day, Bryan sends the dojang's address, as promised.

Good luck, he also texts. **Fair warning: Minjee has a terrifying roundhouse kick. I'm talking about one hit KO level destructive. So, if she tries to kill me for this, save me!!!**

Chapter 23

WHEN I GET TO THE DOJANG, BRYAN AND MINJEE are engaged in intense combat, matching each other's blows perfectly. I never knew Minjee was trained in martial arts, but both she and Bryan are wearing the same protective gear, taekwondo uniform, and black belt.

Neither of them notices me when I come into the room. They're both too engrossed in the fight. Bryan yells as he throws out a high kick, which Minjee expertly parries with her arm before she dodges away.

Bryan texted me to tell me that they're wrapping up ten minutes ago, so I'm confused to see them still fighting. But I'm not complaining. Watching the two of them spar is fascinating, and I can't take my eyes off Minjee. She's graceful and deadly at the same time, while Bryan isn't too bad himself. The two of them move so fast that it's hard to keep up.

Bryan launches into a flying kick, headed directly toward Minjee. I'm about to shout when, in a blink of an eye, Minjee spins and lands a kick right in the middle of his chest.

THWACK!

Bryan falls back onto the mat in a clear KO.

I clap and cheer loudly, caught up in the moment. "Wow! You two were amazing!"

It's only when Minjee glances back at me, her eyes wide in surprise, that I remember what's going on between us. I expect her to say nothing in response, but she stiffly replies, "Thanks. Bryan put up a good fight, though. I'm winded."

She extends a hand to help Bryan up. He takes it and turns his attention to me, giving me a pointed look. "You here to do some training, too?"

I don't miss a beat. "Yeah! I don't have any actual stunts on my own, but I figured I should do *something* to prepare for our scenes next week."

"Well, I'm exhausted," Bryan says. "Gonna go shower. Why don't you train with Minjee for a bit? She's honestly a lot better than me."

Bryan walks away, stopping to give me a thumbs-up when he's out of Minjee's line of sight.

I look back at Minjee, who doesn't meet my gaze.

"Sorry," she says. "I don't know what Bryan's going on about, but I have to go. Have to prep for a photo shoot tomorrow."

I grab her arm as she turns to leave.

"Minjee, wait. Please. Just ten minutes."

She stands there with her back turned toward me, her

shoulders tense, but not moving away.

"What did I do wrong?" I ask. I hate how my voice sounds, so desperate and clingy. But I feel so confused and lost. Even my best acting skills can't hide how I feel right now. "Please, just tell me and I'll leave you alone. I thought we were good friends. I had so much fun with you. But then suddenly . . . I just don't get it. Please, after the years we were friends together, I—"

"It's not your fault, okay?" Minjee cuts me off. She finally turns around to glare at me. Her eyes are shining like they were back at the Bukchon Hanok Village. She looks so upset that I want to reach around to give her a hug. And I would, if I weren't the one making her so sad in the first place. "Look, I . . ." She sniffs before glancing away again. "I need to tell you something. But promise me that you won't tell anyone. If our years of friendship mean *anything* to you, please don't tell anyone."

Minjee's trembling now. My concern for her overshadows my own sadness.

"Wait," I say. "Are you okay? You aren't sick, are you?"

She shakes her head. I reach out to comfort her, but at my touch, she straightens up like she's steeling herself to do something.

Then, she finally meets my eyes.

"I have feelings for you," Minjee says softly. "Whether I like it or not."

Shock runs through my spine.

This is a dream, isn't it? I have to be dreaming. Or maybe I misheard her.

But even as I'm thinking of all this, there's a part of me that isn't so surprised. The warm smiles. The shared looks. The lingering hugs.

Relief floods my thoughts as I realize I wasn't the only one who felt the ever-growing tension between us. But since I just *have* to make sure, I ask, "Wait. You what?"

Minjee flushes. "Never mind. Please just forget what I said."

She's about to run away when I grab her arm, K-drama style.

"Wait, Minjee, this is great! I'm bi!"

Minjee's jaw falls open, her face slack with surprise like mine probably was just moments before. She recovers quickly, though, her expression hardening again as she shakes her head.

"So what? You're dating Bryan."

"Well, actually . . ."

We both turn around to see Bryan standing by the doorway of the dojang, leaning against the frame. He looks in a lot better shape than he did before, all freshened up and his hair still wet from the shower.

"I can assure you that she's not," he continues. "But Hana can explain in more detail."

Minjee steps back, looking so confused that I'm almost concerned that her brain will explode. "Okay, what?"

I sigh. "It was a publicity stunt. For the show. Bryan and I aren't actually dating."

"Although I did like her for a brief period of time," Bryan admits. "But hey, my type is always the people who don't want me back. My one great fatal flaw. Oh well, their loss—"

"Bryan!" both Minjee and I yell in unison. When we realize what we did, we giggle.

"Okay, fine," Bryan says. "I'll leave. For good this time." He turns to Minjee and continues, "Oh, and by the way, to save us some time: I'm pan; Hana knows; and yes, your secret is safe with me. We're all queer. Yay! Okay, bye."

Before either Minjee or I can reply, Bryan runs out of the dojang.

"He's so weird," I say. "Just when I think I understand him, he ends up surprising me all over again."

"You and me both," Minjee replies.

We laugh again. I'm giddy with relief. This current moment feels so nice after all the awkwardness that had built up between us.

"So . . ." Minjee says after a while. "You're bi."

I nod.

"And you're single. Wait, are you trying to tell me that you have feelings for me, too? Is that why all of this is so 'great'?"

My face grows hot. "I don't know when it started, but yeah. I didn't want to ruin our friendship, though, so I didn't say anything."

Minjee bursts into laughter and sinks down onto her knees.

I'm about to ask her if she's okay again when she says, "Same. Well, the being too afraid to say anything, at least. I'm pretty sure I only like girls, though, as much as I didn't want to admit that to myself. But that's a whole other story."

I squeeze her shoulder, just like she did for me when I had my little moment at the hanbok store.

"We can talk about it if you want," I say. "Or we don't have to. Whatever's the most comfortable for you."

"It's just . . ." Minjee trails off and sighs. "I wasn't born in America like you. My parents are more traditionally Korean than anyone I know. I always had a feeling something was *different* about me for quite some time now, since I dated a bunch of guys without really being attracted to them. And when I started having feelings for you . . . well, I was scared. Of this. I still am."

She looks into my eyes. It feels like time's stopped between us, the entire world quiet except my thoughts. My heart beats fast, like it did when I wrapped my arms around Minjee on her motorcycle. Heat rises up in my cheeks again, and in this brief moment in time, all I can see is Minjee and the way she bites her lips, shy and apprehensive.

I swallow, knowing full well what I want to say but still having to fight myself because I don't know if I have enough courage to say it out loud. I've been in relationships with guys before, but this is the first time I've ever confessed my feelings for a girl. And not just any girl, but my best friend.

"I like you," I finally say out loud. "And I'm American, yeah, but my parents are Korean, too. And we're from the South, which is traditionally a pretty conservative part of the States, so . . . I have no idea how they feel about this sort of stuff, either. But I'm willing to figure out everything with you, one step at a time."

Minjee stands up and faces me so our noses are almost touching.

"Okay, one step at a time," she says. "I like you, too."

Before I know what's happening, Minjee's lips are on mine, softly and tenderly at first and then with more force and confidence as I return her kiss.

Chapter 24

I CLOSE MY EYES, FALLING DEEPER AND DEEPER into our kiss with her body pressed against mine and my hands cradling her face.

How could I have ever thought I could stay friends with her?

When we finally break apart, Minjee grins. She's so cute that my heart aches.

"I've wanted to do that for a very long time," she admits.

"Same here," I say.

She rests her forehead on mine. We stay there for a long, quiet moment before pulling away again.

"Oh crap." Minjee points at her taekwondo uniform and protective gear. "I forgot that I'm still wearing this. And I must have been still sweaty, too. Ew."

"It's okay," I reply. "I didn't notice. I was way too distracted by what just happened between us."

Minjee gives me a shy smile, and it's enough to make me want to kiss her all over again.

I can't fully describe the mix of emotions I feel. Part of me is so glad that she feels the same way I do, that it wasn't just me losing my mind over what I thought I sensed between us. But I'm also terrified because I know how big of a deal this is.

Celebrity relationships are kept hush-hush in this industry enough, but a *queer* celebrity relationship is almost unheard of. It's not like Hollywood, where queer couples are relatively more accepted and publicized. If we're not careful, whatever's between Minjee and me could ruin both our careers.

If we do end up dating, we'll have to stay in hiding and be extra careful not to get caught.

I'm uncertain if this is the life I want for either of us.

"What does this mean?" I ask. I want us to be sure if we're really going to do this. "Do you want to date?"

She laughs. "Isn't that obvious?"

"Okay, not going to lie, but I didn't even think you were into girls."

"I didn't think you were into girls, either!" Minjee exclaims in an overly dramatic voice. "Isn't life so funny?"

We laugh together for a little bit before we grow serious again.

"It's not going to be easy," I say. "We're going to have to be careful."

"Yeah." Minjee nods thoughtfully. "But hopefully it'll all be worth it."

She holds out her hand. I take it, this time letting myself fully enjoy just how warm and nice her hand feels in mine.

Minjee gets a mischievous look on her face.

"So," she says, "do you want to spar or not?"

I gulp. I *do* want to try training with Minjee, but I still remember how thoroughly she beat Bryan. And I remember Bryan's warning about her infamous roundhouse kick.

"Only if you promise to *really* go easy on me," I say. "I did karate back in Florida, but I was only a yellow belt."

Minjee gives me a deceivingly innocent smile. "I promise. What kind of pathetic black belt would I be if I beat up a yellow belt? Go ahead and get yourself some protective gear. They're in the closet."

When I finally manage to find gear that'll fit me, Minjee helps me put it on. After I'm all set, I get ready in what I hope is a suitable on-guard stance. "Okay, well. Let's go."

"Hah!" Minjee lets out a yell as she punches the air in front of me.

I parry with a sideways block and try a punch with my other arm. Minjee sidesteps away.

"Good! Maybe I *shouldn't* go easy on you."

"Please do. I don't have a death wish."

"Duly noted."

In slow motion, Minjee kicks in my direction, giving me plenty of time to move away.

"Okay, not *that* easy," I say. I jump forward with a round-house kick.

In a blur of movement, Minjee dodges and hits the floor rolling before jumping back up to pin me down.

For one second, we look into each other's eyes, breathless.

"Was that enough of a challenge for you?" she says, a grin playing on her lips.

And just like that, we're kissing again, fully taking advantage of the fact that we're alone in the dojang.

In the days after, I have to repeatedly remind myself that this isn't all a dream.

You choose our next date location since I chose the last one, Minjee messages me one day, adding a winking emoji at the end.

Oh, so we're counting the Hanok Village day as a date? I grin widely just at the thought.

Yup. And Namdaemun. But I'm counting today as our official day 1.

Things like "this is our day 1" seemed so corny when I saw couples talk about it in K-dramas, but getting that message from someone I care about makes my entire day. I can't stop smiling, and I even catch myself humming when I'm doing my schoolwork later that night.

Since there is so much to do in Seoul, it's hard to choose our next date location, but I ultimately go with the Kakao Friends Flagship Store in Hongdae. I've been obsessively following their official Instagram account for years and always wanted to go but never got a chance. From what I've seen, it seems more like a couples' spot anyway, so I'm excited to go with Minjee.

"I can't believe you've never been there," Minjee says on our way to the store. "Don't you love the Kakao Friends characters? We both use them all the time in our chat!"

"I didn't want to go alone," I admit sheepishly. "People from school always go there on dates."

"True. Well, I'm glad I can go with you now."

In one big dramatic movement, she wraps her scarlet-red scarf around her neck, making me smile. We both agreed to wear more understated clothes during our dates to avoid as much attention as possible, but I'm glad that didn't stop Minjee from adding a touch of her usual flair to her otherwise all-black outfit.

I squeeze her hand, and she gives me a warm smile. I wish I could kiss her right then and there. But I can't. Not in the middle of the street in a popular location like Hongdae.

Hongdae is a bustling nightlife district where students of nearby universities like to hang out. It's also a popular tourist attraction, so there's a bunch of people from all over the world walking in the streets. On my way to meet up with Minjee, I hear people speaking not only Korean but also Mandarin, English, French, and Japanese. People are dressed in everything from the latest Korean street fashion to various school uniforms. Music blasts in the streets, either from the stores' speakers or from the buskers performing live music or dancing K-pop cover dances in front of crowds.

Since Hongdae is *really* packed, both Minjee and I have face masks on to make it harder for people to recognize us. The crowd at Hongdae skews younger, so there's a bigger chance that they watch our show.

We cross the street, and Minjee spreads out her arms in a ta-da pose. "There it is!"

I gasp out loud when I see the store in front of me.

Even from the outside, the Kakao Friends store is super cute, with big-eyed, round characters peering at us from the windows. Currently, the storefront still has decorations up from New Year's. Huge light-up snowflakes fill up the windows, along with the cute animal figures celebrating in different ways.

Minjee laughs at my reaction and gives my shoulder a squeeze.

"Let's go in," she says.

We enter the store. There are endless rows of plushies in all shapes and sizes, from huge ones the size of little kids to tiny keychains. The store has other merchandise, too, like travel pillows and phone cases. And weaving through the products and the different life-size statue photo-op locations are dozens of people either grabbing for merchandise or lining up to take pictures.

"This place is unreal," I say as we get in line to take pictures with a bunny statue.

"Did you know that the bunny character is actually a yellow radish in a bunny costume?" Minjee asks me when we're almost at the front. "Its name is Muzi because it's short for Danmuji, like the word for pickled yellow radish!"

I give the statue a horrified look. The *not*-bunny stares back at me with a wide grin.

"This is why I have trust issues," I say.

Minjee laughs. "You're so ridiculous."

When it's our turn to take pictures, we leave our masks on for obvious reasons. But even with our masks on, we still manage to take a few cute selfies together.

"We should post these later to tell people we were here," Minjee says. "The store will appreciate the shout-out!"

I nod. One perk of us both being girls is that posting pictures from our dates won't cause a riot like photos of Bryan and me did. If anything, everyone would probably think we're just friends and say we're cute. Heteronormativity is annoying, but at least we get *something* good out of it.

"There's also a café at the very top of the store," Minjee says when we're done exploring the first floor. "We can eat something there."

I was hoping we could keep this date relatively private, but when we reach the second floor, a girl approaches us and asks, "Excuse me, are you two Jin Hana and Park Minjee? I'm a die-hard fan of *Fated Destiny* and am so excited for this week's episodes. Can I have your autographs?"

And that's enough to attract the attention of a few other people around us. Minjee and I stop to meet the fans, and the handful rapidly becomes a whole crowd.

"Minjee! Minjee!" shouts a guy, while a girl yells, "Hana!"

Minjee and I share a look.

"Your call," she says. "I'll do whatever you want to do."

I nod, and then slowly, I take off my face mask. Minjee does the same, flashing the crowd a brilliant smile.

"Hey, everyone," she says with a bow, instantly launching into celebrity mode. "I hope all of you are having a good day."

I bow, too, and match her smile. "Thank you for watching our show! Your support means the world to us."

"Are you friends in real life?" asks one of the girls in the crowd.

"It's so cool how you hang out in real life even when you're enemies in the show!" exclaims a guy.

I have to laugh at that one. If only they knew the truth.

But after that, things are relatively chill compared to the other times I got recognized out in public. Some people come up and ask for a selfie or an autograph here and there, but everyone eventually goes back to shopping, giving us space as we continue going through the store.

I breathe a sigh of relief. Interacting with fans doesn't scare me as much as it used to, but it's still nice to be able to spend some uninterrupted time with my girlfriend.

The café on the top floor turns out to be a themed café dedicated to Ryan, my favorite Kakao Friends character. Ryan is a cartoon lion who looks more like a bear with his round face and short tail but is still really cute. I always found his name really hilarious since it's so close in pronunciation to the

English word "lion." Everything from the drinks to the macarons in the café have his face on them.

After much debate, Minjee and I order Ryan-shaped macarons and mango slushy drinks. By then, we have a small group following us, and the barista offers to give us the food on the house. Minjee and I both shake our heads.

"We prefer to pay for ourselves, thank you," I say.

I only refused because I don't like taking free stuff, but the moment I say that, everyone around us cheers.

"You're so cool, Hana!" says one of the girls.

I decide to just go with it. "Thanks!"

Minjee and I sit down at one of the tables with our food. The spots around us fill up instantly, and although Minjee and I can't talk about things as freely as we want to in such a crowded area, it's nice to be able to casually hang out in public.

The sweet, fruity drinks and sugary treats put us in a really good mood, and we're smiling and laughing when we leave the store. By then, it's around ten p.m., and the streets are filled to maximum capacity, so full of people that Minjee and I have to hold hands to stay together. Despite how cramped things are, a thrill goes down my spine. I'm glad the streets are busy enough for us to blend in.

"Hey," Minjee says after a few blocks. "Let's stop by a convenience store. The food was good but kinda too sweet for me. I could use a bottle of water."

"Okay!"

The convenience store we duck into is small and old, with

only two other customers—a college-age couple—browsing the shelves. I follow Minjee to the fridge at the back of the store.

"Why are there so many different brands of water?" Minjee asks, sounding overwhelmed.

"Let's go with these!" I pick two random brands. "That way, we can see which one is better."

"Good plan," Minjee replies with a laugh.

We head to the register, but I linger behind Minjee when one of the college students—the girl—exclaims, "Oppa! Let's take a selfie together. And go out for round-two drinks!"

Her joy makes me smile. As I watch, she flings her arms around her boyfriend, who laughs and hugs her tight.

Minjee circles back to where I'm standing and glances at where I'm looking.

"Aw," she whispers to me. "Young love."

Minjee's comment makes me laugh, since the couple is definitely older than we are.

The college students grab snacks from near the register and get in line in front of us. Even with the bags of chips in their hands, though, they still cling to each other and even share a few kisses, laughing and smiling.

I can't help but feel a prickle of jealousy. *If only I could be like that with Minjee.*

PDA is generally frowned upon a lot more here than it is in the States, but it's sometimes tolerated with hetero couples. It's almost unheard of for same-sex couples to be that overtly affectionate in public, though.

Younger people like us are generally more open-minded and tolerant, but I still have no idea when queer couples will be fully accepted in Korean society. And I have no idea when LGBTQ+ rights will ever become a thing.

I'm still caught up in my thoughts when we pay for our water bottles and leave the store.

"Hey," Minjee says. "Are you okay?"

"Oh, yeah. Sorry, just have a lot on my mind."

"Seems like it. Want to talk about it?"

I'm about to tell Minjee all about my frustrations when I have a sudden epiphany.

I can't do anything to change laws or other people's views, but there *is* one thing I can do.

"I think I'm going to break up with Bryan," I say. "I mean, stop the fake relationship. It's bad enough that we can't ever be public about *our* relationship. I don't want to keep pretending that I'm dating someone else."

Minjee looks alarmed, but she quickly recovers. "You don't have to do that," she says in an even voice. "Especially if keeping up the fake relationship is safer for you. What if the higher-ups object? And fans grow suspicious?"

Those are definitely valid concerns.

"Okay, I'll talk to Sophia about it," I say. "But if she says I can, I'm going to do it. I don't want you to have to see me holding hands with Bryan and acting like we're a couple. *I* don't want to do those things with him. He's a nice guy and all, but he's not you. I should only have to act on-screen."

Minjee gives my hand a tight squeeze. "Okay, I appreciate it. But I want what's safest for you, okay?"

Her concern for me makes my heart ache. I feel so lucky to have her as a girlfriend.

"Okay," I say.

After making sure no one's looking, I give her forehead a kiss.

Chapter 25

SINCE I DON'T WANT TO RISK BEING OVERHEARD on the phone, especially by my parents, I ride the subway early the next morning to Sophia's office before I have to get on set.

My management company looks like any old office building on the outside, but on the inside, it looks like it exists on a whole other plane thanks to its high ceilings, airy open spaces, and golden overhead lights. Every sleek white wall is covered by posters and trophies of various celebrities that the company represents. Some are stars I saw on TV ever since I was a kid, while others are from my parents' time and beyond.

The first time I walked around this building, I felt so inspired by the posters. I relished in the fact that I belonged to the same company as so many great celebrities. But now, I feel like I'm being watched as I walk down the halls.

Sophia hugs me warmly when I enter her office, making me feel a bit better.

She shuts the door behind me and says, "Thanks for coming such a long way, Hana! What did you want to talk about? Must be important if you didn't just want to talk about it on the phone."

Even though I was mentally preparing myself for this the entire day, my hands still grow sweaty. There's a huge lump in my throat, and I take a deep breath so I don't turn around and run out the door.

I close my eyes and just spit it out. "I want to stop fake-dating Bryan. It should be okay, though, right? We haven't gone on a date since New Year's Eve."

Sophia frowns. "It's smarter, professionally at least, to keep it up. Even though it doesn't do much anymore, a lot of the interest in the show started because of your and Bryan's fake relationship. And a lot of the people who shipped you two provide steady viewership for the show. Hana, I definitely want the best for you, and if you're absolutely certain that you want to stop fake-dating Bryan, I'll help you navigate that scenario. But why the sudden change? Did something happen?"

I stare down at my feet. For a moment, I think about how much of the truth I should tell Sophia. I settle on, "I like someone. Actually like them. Things were different when I was single, but now that I'm really dating someone . . . fake-dating someone else feels wrong."

Sophia sighs. She doesn't sound like she's sick of me, more so like she's tired just thinking about the work that's ahead of her. "Okay. That's understandable. Mr. Kim won't be happy with our decision, but sometimes we just have to do what's the best for ourselves."

"If Bryan and I publicly break up before the show is over, wouldn't that garner *more* interest?" I suggest, finally looking up to make eye contact with Sophia. "People might watch the show out of morbid curiosity to see if they can pick up on clues about what 'went wrong' between us."

Sophia purses her lips. "It's risky, but that might work. However, if we're not careful about how we announce it, it might also create lots of unnecessary backlash for you. The last thing you want to do is make an enemy of Bryan's fans."

"Can we maybe work out a joint statement with Bryan's team?"

"Possibly. I'll discuss it with Ms. Ahn and get back to you. Do you by any chance know if Bryan will be okay with you calling off the relationship? Have you talked about it with him yet?"

"Well, not exactly," I admit. "But he knows I like someone else, so I think he'll be fine with it."

"Good to hear. Okay, I'll keep you updated," Sophia promises, pushing her glasses up her nose.

If there's anyone I can trust with all this, it's definitely her.

Sophia didn't pry and politely refrained from asking who I'm dating, but I kind of wish she had. Her . . . my parents . . . I wish I could tell someone the truth about Minjee and me.

On my way back home from set later that evening, I think about coming out to my parents.

They lived in the States for a while before they had me, and in other states, too. Not just Florida, I think to myself. *Maybe they're more open-minded than I think they are.*

But when I open the door to Mom's smiling face and bury myself in her embrace as Dad looks happily on, I lose all my resolve. I couldn't get through anything in my life without my parents there beside me. Even just the smallest possibility that they might not accept me for who I am makes my throat close up in fear.

"You look so tired today," Mom says. "Is everything okay?"

Mom and I keep few secrets from each other, so it pains every fiber of my body to not tell her about what's going on.

"Yeah, everything's fine," I lie. "I guess I'm just worn out after the shooting day."

"Ah, things must be really getting busy in these last few episodes." Mom gives me a sympathetic look. "Hang in there!"

"Thanks, Umma," I say.

"Luckily, the show will finish before the first week of classes, so you should be able to go to school like normal at the beginning of the semester," Mom continues. "Unless you want to take some more time off so you can catch a breath?"

I'm so unprepared for even the thought of going back to school that I immediately say, "Yes, please. If that's okay? I could use a vacation."

"That's true," Mom says. "I'll contact the school and see what we can do!"

Later that night, I'm lying in bed when I get a text from Sophia.

Okay, so Bryan's team agreed to make a joint announcement with us about the breakup. We're going to frame it as a "Bryan moving on from you" thing in order to reduce repercussions for you. I know it's not ideal, but my concern is that if we say anything otherwise, the fans might attack you for "breaking up" with him. Is that okay with you?

I couldn't care less how we "break up," so I reply, **Sure!**

OK. It should go live in an hour or so. I'd mute your notifications if you haven't already.

I'm about to turn off my entire phone when I get a call. I expect it to be Sophia, but it's not. It's Bryan.

"Um, hello?" I ask. "Is everything okay?"

Even though I know Bryan was okay with me dating Minjee, I can't help but feel a little anxious about why he's calling me.

"Oh, hi!" Bryan says. "So, you probably heard about the joint announcement, right?"

"Yeah. We're framing it as a 'you breaking up with me' thing."

"Unfortunately. But yeah, just wanted to give you a heads-up before I post anything. Don't want you to get the wrong idea."

"I won't," I say. "Sophia already explained everything to me, but I appreciate you checking in. Should I unfollow you and block you, too? To up the drama?"

"Ooh, yeah," Bryan replies. "You don't really look at my content anyway, right?"

"Nah."

"Wow, you were really missing out." I don't have to see his face to know he's giving me that mischievous grin of his. "Okay, then, cool. Go ahead and block me on everything. I think they're posting the announcement at nine, so I was thinking of posting my dramatic breakup post at nine thirty. Or maybe ten, since I don't want it to look staged. Are you gonna post anything?"

"Nope. I don't think I would even if we were actually dating."

"Ouch."

"No offense," I quickly say. "I'm just not as public about my private life on social media."

"Yeah, I know. It's cool. I bet my manager *wishes* I were more private."

We both laugh, and I'm expecting Bryan to say bye when he instead adds, "So, just so you know. Between you and me. I think it's incredibly brave what you're doing. Let me know if you need help with anything, okay?"

"Okay," I reply. "Thanks, Bryan. For everything. Let's finish this show strong."

"No problem. And yeah, let's!"

The next morning, my phone miraculously doesn't crash when I turn it back on. It's flooded with texts from friends and news reports about Bryan's and my breakup.

I swipe away all of them for now and go on Bryan's Instagram one last time. His most recent picture, posted at 9:45 p.m. on the dot, is of him on a rooftop with his arms spread wide, his smiling face lit up by the starry skies above.

Free again and it feels so good, reads the caption.

What a lovable jerk. I laugh and block Bryan Yoon on all my social media.

Chapter 26

I FALL INTO A NICE, COMFORTABLE ROUTINE FOR the rest of the month. Our shooting days are busier than ever, but everything goes relatively smoothly. And whenever we have some time off, I hang out with Minjee. We don't have much free time, but when we do, we try to explore as much of Seoul as we can.

In the early morning hours of February first, before we even arrive on set for the day, we get the script for the final episode. As of yesterday, we were halfway into finishing episode nineteen. Usually, we have more time to read the scripts, but to minimize any leaks, Director Cha and the producers waited until the day before we're supposed to shoot it to send it over.

Minjee, Bryan, and I promised each other to not even *peek* at the script before we can all read it together. I'm dying to know who Hyun ends up with, Sora or Danbi. But I somehow manage to resist opening up the PDF of the script until the three of us are sitting at a table in a small but cute café in Ikseon-dong.

"I reserved the café before they open to the public so we'd have some privacy," Bryan explains.

Ikseon-dong is known for its cute cafés and shops, but the one we're at is especially adorable, with bright flowers and plants filling up the space like it's spring and not the dead of winter. The warm light and soft music create a cozy atmosphere, one that's promptly interrupted when Bryan slams down his script on a table and exclaims, "Finally, the moment of truth!"

Minjee and I both jump.

"Jesus," Minjee says. "Do you always have to be so dramatic?"

She shares a look with me, and we giggle.

"Yes," Bryan replies, matter of fact. But he smiles, too.

I take both Minjee's and Bryan's orders and go up to the register.

"I just want to say that I'm *such* a big fan of the show," the barista says as she inputs our order on her tablet. "Do you mind giving us your autographs? We'd love to frame it and hang it in the shop somewhere."

I've seen lots of celebrities' autographs on restaurant walls around Seoul before, but this is the first time a worker ever asked me for one. The thought of my autograph becoming a permanent fixture of a building makes my hands shake just a tiny bit. I'm flattered for sure, but also nervous.

"We'd love to!" I say.

When I return to the table with the barista's pen and paper, Minjee grins at the excited look on my face.

"You're so adorable," she says.

"It's cool now, but wait till you can't go *anywhere* without people shoving papers in your face," Bryan remarks. "Not that I don't appreciate the love. But sometimes I just want peace, you know?"

After we all sign the paper, I take it back to the barista, who bows profusely. "Thank you so much!"

"No problem!"

We wait for the barista to drop off our drinks and leave the room before we open our scripts. Minjee and I start reading at the first page, but Bryan flips to the end.

"Wow!" he says. "I would have never guessed! I can't believe they did that!"

"Shh, don't spoil the ending!" Minjee exclaims.

Bryan smirks, and then we start going over the script, quietly but still passionately reading our parts like we're acting them out. The show's definitely not ending the way I thought it would, but things still get pretty intense. My skin buzzes with adrenaline. My heart races as I flip the page.

"I never thought it'd come to this," Bryan says in character. "I really, really wish I didn't have to do this."

"You have to, Hyun," I plead. "It's our only way out of this."

Holy crap, I think. *Bryan was right. I can't believe what I'm reading. . . .*

"I'm so sorry, Sora," replies Bryan. "I'm so sorry."

There's more of the script, but the three of us sit there in silence for a moment before moving on to the next page.

"Oh my God! They killed you off!" Minjee says to me, growing more heated by the second. "This is ridiculous."

Bryan sits back and takes a sip of his matcha latte. "Definitely an interesting choice on their part."

I'm frozen, still staring at the script. Even though I knew only one of our characters could end up with Hyun, I wasn't expecting Sora to *die*.

"It's okay, guys," I say, even though I'm still trying to process things. "Go ahead and read the rest."

Minjee and Bryan shoot me apologetic looks before continuing on with the rest of the script. Character deaths are rarely personal, but I can't help but feel more than a little bitter. After all, Sora was there first, before the higher-ups decided to tack on a love triangle at the very last minute.

I sip on my rose latte while listening to Bryan and Minjee read.

But then the unthinkable happens.

"No!" Bryan yells out as Hyun. "Not you too!"

I burst out laughing.

"Wait," I say. "Is this real?"

Minjee reads her last monologue and then groans. "Wow,

they really did kill both of us off."

Minjee and I cover our faces with our hands as Bryan finishes the last page on his own.

"Well," he says when he's done. "I know they were trying to make things unpredictable, but . . . this ending is a train wreck."

"The writer really just went, 'Let's kill all the girls!'" Minjee throws up her hands in the air. "Is it too late to quit this show?"

"Unfortunately," I say.

Bryan stands up from his seat. "I would like to apologize on behalf of all men."

"Sit back down," Minjee replies at the same time I say, "Okay, we *cannot* let this air. There's got to be someone we can talk to before we shoot this episode."

"Maybe Director Cha?" Bryan suggests. "Or Mr. Kim?"

"They're probably the ones who okayed this script in the first place," Minjee points out.

"True."

I think back to when Minjee first started on this show, when the two of us came up with a bunch of alternative endings. We were just fooling around, but all those fantasy endings where Sora ends up with Danbi sound *way* better than the real one.

"If they want the ending to be a real surprise, I wish they'd just make things queer or something," I say out loud. "It'd be such a huge step forward in terms of representation, too!"

"Yeah," Bryan agrees. "I'd happily sacrifice Hyun for that ending."

All of a sudden, Minjee gets up from her seat, her face dark with concern. "This is too depressing. I'm gonna go for a walk. Want to come, Hana?"

I glance at Bryan, who shrugs and says, "You two go ahead. I have a commercial shoot before my call time today anyway."

"See you, Bryan," I say.

"See ya."

I catch up with Minjee outside the café. The narrow maze-like alleyways of Ikseon-dong are crowded with people as usual, and we walk by the quaint little shops, marveling at the traditional hanok buildings and the cute storefront displays.

I'm worried about Minjee—I'm worried about all of us, honestly—but I don't say anything. If she's not ready to talk about what's going on, I won't push.

"Come look at these mochi rice cakes!" Minjee exclaims.

We stop at a brightly lit display of mochi rice cakes. The mochi come in all sorts of different flavors, ranging from the standard red bean to cactus and citron. They're really colorful, too. Some are in bright rainbow hues while others are different shades of pastels.

"Let's get a few!" Minjee says. "My treat. I need something sweet to cheer me up after this morning."

Minjee's vague choice of words doesn't escape me. It's probably wise. The shop is crowded, and the last thing we want is someone overhearing us talking about the disastrous last script.

"Okay, thanks!"

We end up picking a bunch of different-flavored mochi, from strawberry to dried persimmons to cookies and cream. At another shop, I buy us some hot tea, and we spend some more time happily snacking as we wander through the alleyways.

Neither of us says anything until we reach a particularly deserted corner.

"What are we going to do about the ending?" Minjee finally asks.

"I have no idea." My mouth still tastes sweet from the mochi, so I sip on my warm barley tea to cleanse my palate.

Minjee sighs. "I'll have to ask my parents about what to do. Hopefully they'll have some advice for us."

It's only then that I'm reminded that, unlike my parents, who would have no relevant experience or advice to help in this situation, Minjee's folks are veterans in the industry. Minjee almost never mentions her folks, so it's very easy to forget.

"Yeah, hopefully we can figure something out."

"But honestly, even if the show ends up sucking, I don't really regret being involved in it, you know?" Minjee says, approaching me. "Because if it weren't for this weird little show, we would have never become a thing."

I look into her eyes. *Fated Destiny* was supposed to be my big break as an actress, the show that would greatly advance my career so I'd no longer get cast as supporting characters. So although I can never just call it a "weird little show" like

Minjee can, I do agree with her on one thing.

"Yeah," I say. "I don't regret us at all."

Minjee leans in for a quick kiss but then suddenly jerks away, staring in shock at someone behind me.

I turn to see a middle-aged man holding a DSLR camera. He's in a hoodie and wearing sunglasses, so I have no idea who he is, but what he was doing is pretty clear. Our eyes meet, and he breaks into a run.

"Hey!" Minjee shouts. "Come back here!"

Sirens go off in my head as I run after him with Minjee. Darting this way and that to avoid crashing into people, we chase after the photographer. But no matter how fast I run, he's faster. My lungs scream with the effort to keep up, and I run and run, but we still lose the man when he turns a corner.

"Crap!" Minjee shouts. She covers her face with her hands. "Oh my God. Hana, I'm so sorry. I never should have . . ."

She breaks down, gasping for breath and falling down to her knees. I nudge her to the side so she's not in anyone's way and wrap my arms around her.

"It's okay," I say, even though my world feels like it's crashing down around me. "It's okay. We'll figure something out."

I hold her tight and really hope I'm right.

Chapter 27

THE REST OF THE DAY GOES BY IN A SLOW BLUR. Every passing second, minute, and hour seem to slug on by as I wait for some breaking news to expose Minjee and me. I called Sophia as soon as I could to tell her what happened, and she said she'd do her best to stop the story from being announced.

"But I can't guarantee that I can block them," Sophia warned me. "The biggest problem is that we don't know who this guy was or who he's working for. The best we can hope for is that he won't go public with the picture he took. A lot of times these people ask for compensation first."

But as it turns out, we don't have to worry about the news breaking after all. One hour before we're supposed to be on set, I get an email from the studio.

PRODUCTION OF "FATED DESTINY" TO BE SUSPENDED, EFFECTIVE IMMEDIATELY, says the subject line.

I break into a cold sweat as I open the email. Thankfully, it doesn't say much, but it says enough, explaining how "due to unforeseen circumstances," Mr. Kim has decided to temporarily suspend production of our show. It also says that both Minjee and I should "report to Mr. Kim ASAP" with our managers.

Bryan's the first to text both of us.

BRYAN YOON: OKAY, WTF is going on? Did something happen after you two left?

PARK MINJEE: Long story. Will explain later.

ME: Sorry, Bryan. Heading over to talk to Mr. Kim now. We'll tell you everything as soon as we figure out what's going on.

PARK MINJEE: Same. See you there.

Sophia, Minjee, and Minjee's manager—Mr. Baek, I think his name is—are all waiting for me when I get to the company building in Sangam-dong. Everyone's faces are grim, and Sophia puts a hand on my shoulder as we enter the building.

"Okay, kiddo, deep breaths," she says. "It could be worse."

Mr. Baek lets out a sharp laugh and takes off his sunglasses.

"We can only hope that Mr. Kim is feeling generous," he says.

Sophia and Mr. Baek go back and forth a little bit, but I tune them out to focus on Minjee, who's keeping her eyes on the floor as we walk to the elevator.

When the doors close and we're on our way up, I take Minjee's hand and squeeze it. "Hey."

"Hey," she says back, completely stone-faced. "Sorry for all of this."

"It's okay," I say. Even though I have no idea how things

are going to play out, I'm certain about one thing: I don't blame Minjee for any of this. "You were just caught up in the moment. It happens. We're in this together, okay?"

"Okay." Minjee's bottom lip trembles, and she bites it before squeezing my hand back. "Thanks."

When we enter Mr. Kim's office, he angrily stares us down from his massive dark mahogany desk. Photos of Minjee and me on various dates are spread out on his desk, with the last one being the one of Minjee kissing me from earlier today.

"You had them *followed*?" Sophia asks in horror. She's the first of us to put it together, and the only one who can manage to express her horror out loud. If she's surprised about seeing Minjee and me together in those photos, she doesn't show it. Sophia keeps her attention laser-focused on Mr. Kim.

"Of course," Mr. Kim says, matter of fact. "I hired a private investigator to follow Bryan and the two girls. Teenagers can be a lot of trouble. The last thing I wanted was a scandal to break out during the show. My actors are expected to uphold the reputation of my company, after all. It was just supposed to be a routine surveillance, but then one of my men found *this*."

He points at the last photo.

"Do you know how fortunate you two are that it was *my* private investigator that took the photo of you two like this and not some paparazzi?" he asks Minjee and me, seething. "If this story got out, all hell would break loose. This isn't *America*," he adds, glaring pointedly at me. "I hope you realize this."

Sophia steps in front of me, gently but firmly pushing me behind her.

"I can assure you that my client is very much aware of the norms of Korean society. There is a reason why Hana's not out publicly."

Mr. Baek joins in. "My client is aware of them as well, despite her rashness."

Minjee gives Mr. Kim a full bow. "I'm so sorry, Mr. Kim," she says. "Please, it was me who was foolish, not Hana. If you're going to be angry, please be mad at me."

"I am displeased with both of you." Mr. Kim leans back in his leather armchair. "Not only does your relationship jeopardize the reputation of my company, but it goes against the values of myself as well as many respectable members of our community. I have every right to terminate your contracts and remove you from the show."

"Well, you're doing that no matter what, aren't you?" I blurt out, unable to keep quiet any longer. "We read the final script. You killed both of our characters off."

"Hana," hisses Sophia. "Please."

Mr. Kim raises his eyebrows and interlaces his fingers in front of him on his desk.

"Ah yes, Hana-ssi," Mr. Kim says, his voice dangerously low. "Having you on the show was definitely a calculated risk on my part. I wasn't sure about having an American on board, but Director Cha assured me you were the best fit for the role."

I make a mental note to bring Director Cha a gift if we

ever resume shooting. He's so tough-love with us on set that it's hard to remember that underneath the grumbling and mean-mugging, he's a nice guy.

Mr. Kim looks out at all of us. "In any case, I have a proposition. The show is almost over, after all, so it's probably best we continue."

Minjee and I share a look. Could he really be letting us go on with the show?

"But," Mr. Kim says sharply, pointing at first Minjee and then me. "*This* cannot continue. End your relationship at once or I will permanently cease production of the show. I cannot have you two gallivanting around in an immoral fashion. Yes, halting the show without properly completing it would be a major inconvenience on the company, but it is a smaller price to pay compared to the drastic consequences of the public finding out about you two."

I'm about to protest when Sophia steps in front of me again.

"Understood," she says. "I will discuss things with my client and let you know of our decision. I'm assuming you will require Hana and Minjee to sign some sort of legal document agreeing to cease their relations?"

Mr. Kim harrumphs. "Of course. It's not like you can trust kids these days."

"My client and I will let you know as well," Mr. Baek says after a pointed look from Sophia. "Have a good day, sir."

Sophia practically steers the three of us out of Mr. Kim's office and into a nearby conference room.

"Okay," she says after shutting the door behind us. "So at least he's giving us an ultimatum."

"At least?" I hiss. "He's a crusty old homophobe! How is anything he said a good thing?"

Mr. Baek scoffs. "Please control your client, Miss Sophia. She should recognize a generous proposition when she sees one."

Sophia fixes Mr. Baek with a steely glare, making him shrink back like a turtle in its shell.

"Never tell me how to handle my clients," she says. "And may I remind you that it's the rash behavior of *your* client that got us in this mess in the first place?"

They look like they're about to bicker again, so I spread out my hands in a gesture of peace. "Look, guys. I know I'm American and whatever, but Mr. Kim really can't do this to us, right? He can't just stop a show when we're so close to being finished?"

Mr. Baek scoffs. "You don't get it, do you? He owns a huge chunk of the company, so he can do whatever he wants. And it's not uncommon for entertainment company heads to shut down a relationship. You forget that in the music industry, companies ban their talent from dating, period."

I look down at my feet, remembering what Bryan said about his K-pop contract forbidding him from actually dating anyone.

"So that's it, then?" I ask. "We can't do anything?"

Minjee speaks up then, after remaining quiet this entire time. "Hana, I appreciate how much you care about us. And believe me, I care too. But I can't help but think of the cast and crew members who will be affected if the show randomly gets canceled like this. So maybe it's best if we break up."

Pain shoots through my chest. I understand what Minjee is saying, but I still can't stop the hurt.

This can't be how our relationship ends, I think. *We just started dating!*

I slowly shake my head.

"No," I say. "I mean, okay, I agree. We shouldn't let the show get canceled, especially when so many people depend on it. But I'm not letting him win so easily. There's got to be some way!"

No one says anything for a few beats, and Sophia's phone chirps.

"It's Mr. Kim," she says. "He said he's giving us forty-eight hours. If, at the end of forty-eight hours, you and Minjee don't sign the legal document agreeing to break up, he's going to officially cease the production of *Fated Destiny*."

Chapter 28

AFTER OUR MANAGERS LEAVE, MINJEE AND I CALL Bryan and put him on speakerphone.

"Yikes on a bike," he says in English after we explain the situation to him. If things weren't so dire, I'd tell him no one actually uses that expression. "So, forty-eight hours is *not* a lot of time, but I know a few people that might be able to help. Go home for now. I'll let you know what they say."

"Okay," I say. "Thanks, Bryan."

"Yeah, thanks," says Minjee.

I hug Minjee one last time before heading back home. My parents aren't in yet—today is one of their working-late days—so I sit alone in front of the TV.

It's a weeknight, so the only things on air right now are melodramas meant for older viewers and reruns of episodes that already premiered.

I switch through the channels and stop when I find a rerun episode of *Fated Destiny*. It's the episode where Minjee's character and I first clash against each other at the palace. The day we shot that scene seems like such a long time ago, even though it's only been a little over a month. Everything's so fast-paced in the K-drama production world that it really messes up my perception of time.

When we shot the scene, I was only thinking about Minjee and how cold it was. Today, as I watch the episode on TV, I focus on myself. Every expression flickers on my face so rapidly, and I still feel all of Sora's emotions as if they were my own.

I remember how excited I was when I was first cast in this show, how passionate I was about my role and how thankful I was of the huge opportunity. Somewhere along the way, I lost all that, weighed down by the intense shooting schedules and drama both on and off set.

I wish I could go back to how things were when I first started the show, but I know that's not possible. Even if we did somehow get everything with Mr. Kim figured out, there's still that horrible last script.

The episode ends, and I make myself take deep breaths.

One thing at a time, I think to myself. *Everything will work out.*

When my parents come home a few hours later, it's absolute torture to not be able to tell them what's going on. But I can't. It's impossible not to confide in them without telling them about Minjee and me. I wish I were out to them so they could help me figure out what to do.

Not wanting to just sit still and do nothing, I text Bryan.

Did you hear anything back from your friends yet?

Bryan responds immediately.

Yeah! Was actually just about to message you and Min-jee. Let's all meet back at the café we were at tomorrow? Don't know where else would be safe to talk.

Hope flickers inside of me, like a candle lighting up a dark room. I agree to meet my friends there before going to sleep that night, carefully guarding that small glimmer.

Bryan is the only person sitting at the café when Minjee and I enter through the doors the next morning. At first, I almost don't recognize him.

Instead of being his usual flashy, colorful self, he's dressed down in a black turtleneck and gray pants. He's more pale and solemn than I've ever seen him, and even with sunglasses covering his eyes, I can tell how tense he is by his scrunched-up shoulders and tapping fingers.

Bryan takes off his shades when we sit down, and I see the exhaustion in his dark circled eyes. The three of us all look bone-tired. I feel like I've gotten ten years older in the last twenty-four hours.

"So," Bryan says, "I asked around in my friend circles about our current situation. I didn't give them the exact details of course, but I just asked if anyone had similar experiences with being bullied by an executive or whatnot."

"And?" Minjee asks, biting her lip.

"Well, one of them had a similar experience in the K-pop world. She said she had a hard time breaking into the industry because of some bullying, but she managed to get past that because she stood up for herself and a lot of people backed her up. Like, fans and such."

"So . . . are you saying we should go public with what's going on?" I ask, feeling both really inspired and terrified at the same time.

Bryan hesitates, scratching his head before replying, "Well, whether you do is entirely up to you, of course. But it *is* one possibility. I think nowadays people our age are also a lot more tolerant about queer stuff, even though a lot hasn't changed government-wise in Korea since old people still run things. It's a huge risk for sure, but maybe it's worth it?"

I think back to how alone I felt when I got home yesterday, about how I wished more people like my parents knew I was bi so I could get some kind of support. I'll probably get a lot of homophobic backlash online, but surely Mom and Dad would accept me for who I am? I'm terrified that I'll end up getting rejected, but maybe Bryan is right. Maybe some people *will* back us up.

"We could issue a statement," I say, looking to Minjee and Bryan. "Just explaining what's going on. I'm sure lots of people around the world would be upset if they knew the truth. Especially the viewers of our show in more tolerant countries."

"Okay, I hate to play the devil's advocate here," Bryan says, "but since this is kind of my idea, I feel obligated to remind you that this is really risky. In the process of doing all this, you and Minjee would have to come out. Are you willing to do that? Do your families even know you're queer? Full disclosure, but I really can't come out anytime soon. Yeah, there are queer K-pop stars that are out like Holland, but my folks probably won't be okay with it. They're really conservative and homophobic."

I look down at my hands. I'm so afraid at just the thought of coming out to my parents, but some part of me is hopeful since nothing they've said in the past has made me believe that they're homophobic. But then again, they also haven't said anything in support of LGBTQ+ rights, either.

"You're right. I need to check in with them first before I do anything publicly."

I look to Minjee. She's as pale as a sheet.

"You okay?" I ask.

"Yeah," she says when our gazes meet. "But I need to talk to my parents, too. They're pretty traditional, so there's a good chance they won't take it well."

Bryan sighs. "I really wish you two weren't under such a huge time crunch."

I shake my head. "Honestly, I've wanted to come out to my parents for a long time now."

"Things would definitely be a lot easier if we didn't have to sneak around behind our parents' backs," Minjee agrees. But she still looks pretty scared.

I take her hand. "We don't have to do this if you don't think this is a good idea. Or I can just say I'm the one that has a crush on you. You won't have to come out at all."

Minjee shakes her head. "No," she says. "I can't let you do that. Plus, it's about time my parents knew I'm not interested in guys at all."

Bryan sits back in his chair. "I guess it's decided, then. Sorry I can't come out, too. I want to, for solidarity's sake."

I shake my head. "No, it's okay. Safety first. If you for sure know your parents won't be okay with it, then you shouldn't."

"Yeah," Minjee agrees. "Just have our backs during the fallout."

Bryan rapidly nods. "Of course. Let me know if I can help with anything."

I pull Bryan and Minjee in for a tight hug, wishing I knew everything was going to be okay.

Chapter 29

WHEN MY PARENTS RETURN HOME FROM WORK that night, I give them both long, big hugs. Mom and Dad look surprised, but they hold on tight to me anyway. I have no idea if they'll let me hug them like this ever again, so I take in the warmth and comfort as much as I can.

Then, I step back, take a deep breath, and say, "Umma, Appa, I have something I need to tell you."

Their eyes go wide in concern.

"Hana, are you okay?" Mom says. "Whatever it is, you can tell your appa and me. No secrets between us, right?"

Dad looks equally worried, but he just nods along.

"You two better take a seat," I say.

We walk over to the living room, and I wait for my parents to get situated on the couch.

When I don't say anything for a long time, Dad blurts out, "Are you pregnant?"

I go crimson. "Appa! No!"

My parents both let out huge sighs of relief.

I decide to just get it over with. My heart pounding in my ears, I say, "But I am bi." I rack my brain for the Korean word for it, something I googled while getting ready for this talk. "Yang-sung aeja. I like both guys and girls."

My parents grow completely still. The entire room is so quiet that I can hear the water dripping from our kitchen faucet. *Drip. Drip. Drip.*

They stare at me, and I brace myself for my parents' reactions.

But then, Mom bursts out laughing.

"Hana," she says. "We already know. Well, for the longest time your appa and I thought you might be lesbian before you started talking about some of the boys at school. But your strongest crushes were always on your female classmates, so we figured you were more into girls. The way you'd talk about your friend Minjee . . . you were obsessed!"

Dad nods again.

"Wait, you guys *knew*?" I say, filled with a mix of shock and relief. "Even *I* didn't know I liked Minjee in that way back then. Why didn't you ever say anything?"

Mom shrugs. "We didn't want to assume too much, just in case. And more importantly, we wanted you to tell us only when you were ready."

"Okay," I say, letting out a quick breath. My heart's still

beating super fast, but it doesn't feel like it's about to explode anymore. "Well, Minjee is my girlfriend now, officially. And I have a lot more things to catch you guys up on."

My parents' facial expressions range from surprise to anger to horror as I tell them everything that's been going on for the past few weeks.

Mom gasps when I tell her about the show's possible cancellation. "Can they do that?"

I shrug. "Part of me hopes Mr. Kim's just bluffing, but he also said he'd be willing to pay for all the repercussions of canceling the show, because to him, that's better than having us finish it. He's really homophobic."

Dad nods. "I'm not surprised. A lot of my friends are. One of them has a gay son and repeatedly says that he hopes the military will 'turn him straight.'"

Knowing how close-minded some people are, what Dad said isn't surprising, but it still makes me feel sick.

"Wait," I say. "If a lot of your friends are homophobic, then why aren't you?"

I have no idea if this is even an appropriate question to ask, but I can't help but be curious.

Dad hesitates and looks at Mom, who nods at him. He then slowly says, "I wouldn't consider myself to be totally accepting. To be honest, your umma and I . . . we are still cut from the same cloth as Mr. Kim and that older, less-accepting generation. It's very difficult for me to understand. But even though we can't exactly understand it, we will always care more about you and your happiness."

This is the most I've heard Dad say in a while. I'm still processing everything he's said when Mom adds, "We love you, Hana. No matter what."

Dad nods. I'm full-on bawling as I launch myself at my parents for another big group hug. Mom laughs again, and the three of us embrace for a long time.

"So," Mom says when we break apart. "What do you plan on doing about Mr. Kim?"

Mom's and Dad's faces go sheet white when I tell them that I plan to publicly come out.

"Honey," Mom says, "I understand why you want to make this kind of statement and will support you no matter what, but you do realize that by doing all this, you might jeopardize your chances of ever getting hired in another show or movie in Korea, right? There's no telling how people will react to your words, and the risks are big. You are still young. You have a whole future ahead of you. Are you sure you don't want to just let all of this blow over?"

I think about earlier today and how out of the three teens in our friend group, I'm the only one who felt relatively safe about coming out to my parents. Who knows how many of us are really out there, in the Korean entertainment industry and beyond? People see queerness as such an anomaly, as if there aren't that many of us. But what if we're actually the norm, and we're all just in hiding?

Something deep inside me tells me I'll forever regret it if I don't make this statement now. Regardless of what *might* happen with my career.

"Yeah," I say. "I am. I may be just starting out, but if this industry isn't okay with who I am, then I don't want to keep working in it anyway."

Mom looks intently at my face for a long moment and then sighs. "All right. Well, like I said before, we support you no matter what."

She wraps me into a hug. Dad lingers behind for a few seconds before also slowly coming around to embrace Mom and me again. I try to harness the gratitude and love I feel now so I can remember it when I'll need it the most.

When I feel ready to break apart from my parents, I walk into my room and call my manager.

"Sophia?" I ask.

"Yes?"

"I want to make a public statement telling the truth about what happened so everyone knows about what Mr. Kim is trying to do now."

Sophia doesn't say anything for a few seconds after I explain to her what I want to say. I'm afraid she's hung up, when she finally replies, "Hana, from a professional perspective, I can't advise you to follow this course of action. It's a huge risk, career-wise, just because of how people might react. You might not get another show or movie in this industry again."

"I know. I already talked to my parents about it, and that's what they said, too."

"Yes, I figured as much." She lets out a short sigh and continues, "But on a personal level, I know why you feel the need to do this and why this is important for you. Even though I manage your career, I also care about your personal well-being and happiness. So if you're absolutely sure about making this sort of statement, despite the risks, I'll set up a press conference for you."

"How about you? Wouldn't me issuing this statement hurt you career-wise as well?"

"Well, yes, probably."

"You're more than welcome to say I forced you into this. I don't want to risk your career, too, especially not after you've been so good to me."

Sophia laughs. "No, I wouldn't allow that. I can handle whatever comes next. Don't you worry about me."

"Sophia . . . thank you."

"No problem. Just be sure to send me a transcript of what you want to say so I can look over it before the actual conference. And make sure Minjee and her team are okay with you coming out, since this directly impacts her, too."

"Will do."

As soon as I hang up, I text Minjee, asking her how things went with her parents.

I expect her to respond right away, like she always does.

But first minutes and then hours pass with no response from Minjee.

I try calling her. Straight to voice mail. I call again. Nothing changes.

Even though I'm anxiously worried about Minjee, I start working on my statement since we're so pressed for time. My parents help, and so does Bryan over text and video chat. By the end of the day, I have the statement ready to send to Sophia and Minjee.

I'm about to go to bed when I get a call.

When I pick up, the other line is completely silent. I'm wondering if it's a butt dial when Minjee says, "I came out to my parents. And it didn't go well."

Her voice is raw, like she's spent the last several hours crying. My chest immediately tightens, hurting from the pain in her voice.

"Do you need anything?" I ask. "Are you safe?"

"Yeah," Minjee says breathlessly. "I'm just exhausted. We've been arguing nonstop all day. They finally went to bed a few minutes ago. Honestly, I consider myself lucky they didn't kick me out. I have no idea what my parents are planning to do, but at least I have a roof over my head. I know a lot of kids who came out and weren't so lucky."

Her voice breaks at the end, and hearing her cry makes my own eyes tear up.

"We don't have to go through with this," I say. "If you just want to lie low or think it's better for you to not come out publicly, we don't have to do this. I can scrap my statement and we can go back to filming the rest of the show. Just say the word."

"No," Minjee replies, almost immediately. "Things have to change. We have to at least try."

I wish she were next to me so I could kiss her and hug her tight.

"You're so brave," I say. "Seriously, if you need anything at all, a safe place to stay, someone to talk to . . . don't hesitate to let me know. I love you."

It's only after I say it that I realize I've never said those words to her before.

Minjee lets out a quick breath. "I love you, too. Now, let's bring down the homophobic patriarchy."

Chapter 30

EARLY NEXT MORNING, THERE'S A KNOCK AT OUR apartment door. When I open it, I see Minjee and Bryan standing at my front step. Both have sunglasses on and their jacket hoods up for the sake of anonymity, and so do I. We all look like we're embarking on some secret mission. And I guess in a way we are. If we weren't in such a rush, I'd snap a quick selfie of us to commemorate how badass we look.

"So," Bryan says, "you ready for this thing?"

In the end, the three of us combined our statements so we could make one big general announcement to the public during the press conference that our managers set up for us.

I pull Bryan and Minjee in for a hug before we head downstairs.

"Yup," I say. "Let's go."

Sophia is waiting for us at the parking lot in the company car.

"All right, here we go," she says when we get in.

On the way to the studio, Minjee grabs my hand and squeezes it in a reassuring way. No one speaks during the entire car ride, and I take the moment to rehearse in my head what I want to say. I got my part of the statement approved by Mom, Sophia, and Minjee before I memorized it. I practiced it countless times after that, but I still feel like I can't go over it enough.

As is true for most public statements, I know we'll only have this one chance to give everyone the most accurate picture of what happened. With how fast social media spreads things, one wrong word or gesture and I might just become the next pop culture meme. The pressure only gets worse as we approach the station. Soon enough, it gets hard to breathe.

I reach out toward Minjee. She immediately leans her head against my shoulder.

"Sorry to ruin your little K-drama moment, but you haven't forgotten that I'm here in the car with you guys, right?" Bryan asks, sounding more amused than annoyed.

"Bryan," Minjee says, sitting up straight to face him. "We should get you a boyfriend. Or a girlfriend. Or a nonbinary partner. Anyone! Aren't you sick of being the third wheel?"

"Obviously. But hey, who said I'm not dating anyone?"

Minjee and I look at each other with our eyebrows raised.

"Wait, what?" I ask.

Bryan scoffs. "Oh, come on. I have a life outside of the show, too, you know. It's fairly new, though. I learned a *lot* from Hana's and my fake relationship, so . . . yeah. Trying my best to keep it a secret from everyone for now."

"Isn't it wild how much power the industry has over our personal lives?" I ask, suddenly exhausted. "I mean, the fact that we're having to make this statement at all . . ."

"Yeah," Minjee replies. "But we've got this. I know you guys are scared. Believe me, I am, too. But we'll get through this, okay? And think about the countless people out there who need to hear what we have to say."

I nod and force myself to relax, thinking about the conversation I had with Minjee last night. In the end, I switch to the acting part of my brain, because it's easier to *pretend* I'm someone else who's unafraid than to calm myself down.

Just because I'm scared, doesn't mean the world has to know it, I remind myself.

When we get to the TV station, the producer greets us with a firm nod. "This way. They're ready for you."

Both Ms. Ahn and Mr. Baek join us then, and the six of us enter the conference room. Cameras start flashing almost instantly. Reporters excitedly chatter among themselves or yell questions directly at us.

"Don't answer any of them," Sophia hisses. "Ignore them for now and just go up to the stage. We'll do a Q and A later, so don't let any of them interrupt your statement."

She takes the lead, with us following her and the other two managers protecting our backs as we step onto the stage. Three chairs wait for us in that wide-open space, with bottles of water placed thoughtfully on the seats.

Sophia waits for us to sit down before looking out at the sea of reporters. Ever the face of bravery, she fiercely meets their gazes and says, "Everyone, hello, my name is Sophia Min. I'm Hana's manager. I would like to ask all of you to please not misconstrue anything that is said today. If you spread false information, I and the other managers present today will press charges. Also, please remember that the statement is a reflection of the teens' own personal beliefs and interests and not their companies' nor the studio's. Thank you."

When she's done addressing the reporters, Sophia comes over to give us each a mic.

"Best of luck," she tells us before leaving the stage to join the other managers sitting at the front of the audience.

We agreed that Bryan and I should have most of the limelight, since our fake-dating scheme is what started this whole mess in the first place. It also seems like the best way to protect Minjee, since she's already dealing with a lot from her family.

So I'm the first to bring the mic up to speak.

As I look out at the crowd, I'm hit by an overwhelming desire to stand up for myself and my friends. Even though it may not be what people expect me to do, I can't just passively accept things for the way they are now. I'm not going to just sit there and let decisions be made for me.

"Good morning," I say, speaking slowly so my Korean comes out clearly and coherently. "We're here today to publicly address the suspension of *Fated Destiny*. Bryan, Minjee, and I have a lot to tell you all about, so please save your questions for the end."

The camera flashes intensify, and there are more shouts from the reporters. I press on, clutching the side of my chair with my free hand. "First of all, Bryan and I never dated in real life. We were pressured by the adults in the industry to enter into a fake relationship for public attention. We're good friends but nothing more than that."

There's an uproar from the reporters. Several people shout, "Bryan! What do you have to say to that?" and "Is this true, Bryan?"

Bryan picks up his mic and says, "Yes. I apologize to all my fans, but my relationship with Hana wasn't real. Honestly, the only real relationship I have is the one I have with the Brybabies, who will always be number one in my heart."

He flashes everyone a brilliant smile and makes a heart with his thumb and forefinger. Bryan's stereotypically K-pop prince response makes me want to throw up a little, but I also feel an urge to laugh. And I would have, too, if our current situation weren't so serious.

I glance back at Minjee for one last time before I say the next part. She nods.

"And that's not the only thing we kept from all of you," I say. "The reason why *Fated Destiny* was temporarily suspended is because it was recently discovered by a higher-up at our company that I am in a relationship with my costar Park Minjee."

If I thought people were upset about Bryan and me, it's

nothing compared to how loud and chaotic the room is now. So many voices yell at once that I can't hear myself think.

"He had us followed," I continue, practically shouting to be heard, "by a private investigator and threatened to cease production of the show and cancel it outright if Minjee and I didn't break up. We're just two kids in love! Why should it matter so much if we're both girls?"

I bow, deeply and more sincerely than I ever have in my entire life.

"I apologize to everyone for not being honest. But we were all afraid to tell the truth." I look straight into one of the main news cameras, thinking of the viewers back home. My parents are probably watching right now, with Mom tightly clutching Dad's hand and Dad biting his lip. I gather strength from the fact that they're probably listening to every word I'm saying as I continue. "I know Korean society is different from how things are like in the US. And I understand if you think how I live my life is wrong. But I kept this secret about who I am for so long, even to my parents, who are the most important people in my life. And I know there are countless other teens out there who have a secret like me, too. So I can't just sit here and be quiet anymore."

I finally look at Minjee again. She doesn't say anything, but the tears in her eyes are more than enough.

"Times are changing. In a recent study, around forty-four percent of Koreans said queer people should be accepted by society. Of those, over three-quarters of young people said they supported us, even though most of the older population didn't." I look straight into one of the cameras. "So please, support your queer friends and family. And if you're queer, love yourself. Please don't subscribe to outdated values. Young people like you and me can make a difference. We need to stand up for what we think is right."

To my surprise, there are a few claps from the audience, which is more support than I expected. When it's quiet again, Minjee and Bryan come in after me, reiterating what I said and adding their own personal details about what happened. When we're done, almost every reporter in the room raises their hand to ask follow-up questions. We answer a couple, but then our managers step up to the stage and end the conference.

Sophia gives me a quick hug before ushering me off the stage.

"You did great," she whispers in my ear. "Now let me handle the rest."

I nod and leave the stage with Minjee and Bryan. The conference went better than I expected, but only when Minjee and I hug in the hallway outside the conference room do I feel like I can breathe again.

Chapter 31

ARTICLES AND RECORDINGS FROM OUR PRESS conference hit the internet before it's even officially over. Overall, the responses are mixed, with more people supporting us than I thought they would. But even those who don't support our beliefs agree that it was wrong of Mr. Kim to have Minjee and me followed. The studio releases a statement saying that they're going to put Mr. Kim's actions "under review."

Even though Sophia suggested that I not check social media for the time being, I end up going on my phone anyway. The *not knowing* what people are saying bugs me so much that I can't sleep. I log on to my accounts in the middle of the night.

The moment I do, I feel like I'm getting yelled at by millions of voices. On Twitter, trolls meme the heck out of our show, posting screenshots with "alternative lines" and other content about how they can't take the show seriously anymore because the love triangle is a sham. In my Instagram comments, I see people either applauding Minjee and me or saying we should be ashamed of ourselves. Homophobic haters spam me on Twitter and other social media, saying that I should "retire" from the industry. People on opposing sides break into fights on various sites, with lots of insults and mean comments exchanged in between.

The silver lining in the midst of all this chaos is the countless DM requests I receive from closeted people in South Korea and other countries all over the world saying what an inspiration I am to them. Although I have no idea how all of this will affect my own life yet, this alone is enough for me to know I made the right choice.

I expect the coverage of our conference to die down over the weekend, but the opposite happens. International news outlets pick up our story and start reporting on it all over the world. International LGBTQ+ activists and queer celebrities tell me they support me, and a lot of Hollywood people even say they'd be happy to work with me one day.

Even though the support doesn't nullify the pain of the hurtful comments, I'm still grateful for whatever support I can get.

The following Monday, Bryan sends out a message in our group chat.

BRYAN YOON: Sooo, I don't know about you guys but things have been ROUGH. Luckily my fans seem to be taking it mostly well though. They seem happy I was single this whole time lol. Anyway, who's down for some good food?

I don't think I've ever been happier to hear from Bryan.

ME: YES PLEASE! What were you thinking?

PARK MINJEE: I'm down too 👀

BRYAN YOON: OK, I'm personally craving jjajangmyeon. We'll probably have to get it delivered to someone's place though cuz I don't think it's a good idea for any of us to be seen out in public right now.

I text my mom, who's at work but instantly replies with the thumbs-up emoji when I ask if I can have friends over.

ME: You guys can come to my place!

BRYAN YOON: Let's go!!!!

PARK MINJEE: 🙌

That evening, Minjee and Bryan come over to my apartment. Bryan arrives first, and initially, I'm self-conscious about our slightly messy and smaller-than-average apartment. It's been a while since I've been this acutely aware of the fact that he's an internationally famous K-pop superstar.

But if Bryan thinks any less of me because of where I live, he doesn't show it. Instead, he quickly makes himself at home, flopping down onto the couch like he owns the place.

I roll my eyes. Typical Bryan.

Any remaining thoughts I have of Bryan disappear when Minjee arrives. She's wearing an avant-garde blue dress that has huge yet somehow still stylish ruffles around the collar. Along with her bold, vibrant makeup, she looks *amazing*. It's so nice to see her dressed like her usual self again.

"Hi," I say, giving her a hug.

"Hey." She returns my hug, lingering a bit to squeeze my arm when we pull away. "How are you?"

I shrug. "I think we've all been better. But that's why we're here, right?"

"Yup!" Bryan cuts in. "And I'm *starving*, so let's order some food already!"

Minjee and I both jump before bursting out laughing. For a few seconds, we really were in our own little world.

We end up ordering jjajangmyeon and jjamppong, along with sweet and sour pork.

Like pretty much all delivery in Korea, our food comes super fast.

After setting the food down on the dining room table, we open the containers. The black bean noodles and spicy seafood noodle soup smell amazing. My mouth instantly starts watering.

"Oh God," says Minjee. "Okay, today is going to be my cheat day of the week."

We used Bryan's delivery app, so I ask, "How much do we owe you, Bryan?"

Bryan gives me a smug smile. "Don't worry about it. Oppa's got you covered."

Minjee and I both give Bryan a death glare.

"I told you never to use oppa like that ever again!" I reply, just as Minjee says, "Wait, you're older than us? You don't look it."

"Yup," Bryan says. "I'm a year older than both of you.

Although, if you really want me to, I can call you 'Noonim.'"

"Noonim" is the really formal version of the word for "older sister" in Korean. Minjee shoots him a look that could break glass.

"No way!" Minjee says. "That makes me feel way too old. Unlike Hana, I'd be *happy* to call you Oppa."

We all burst into laughter at that.

"Come on," I say when we've calmed down. "Let's dig in."

The food is just as good as it smells, and it puts everyone in a good mood. By the time we finish eating, we've talked about all sorts of things from our different tastes in movies to our dreams about the future.

"I want to try directing one day," Bryan says. "Cone of silence, but that's the real reason I took a break from NOVA. Traveling around the world and performing for fans is fun and all, but I know a lot of that will go away when I get older. And what will I have then? What if I go serve my time in the military and come back to no one knowing who I am?"

I've always heard Korean male celebrities worry about the compulsory two-year military service, since it's nearly impossible to get an exemption from that rule, no matter how famous you are. Even BTS only managed to get their service requirements delayed. In an industry that's always rapidly changing and moving on to the next big thing, being away for two years is frightening.

"That's a valid fear," Minjee says. "Are you using this role as a way to break into the film industry?"

"Basically, yeah," Bryan says. "I've always loved movies and TV shows. After long training days and exhausting concerts, watching stuff is how I always wound down at night. Don't laugh, but I was also really inspired by Bong Joon Ho and how he made the world pay attention to Korean cinema by winning all those prestigious international awards. I know a lot of people probably won't take me seriously at first, especially since they only know me as a K-pop star. But maybe someday they will."

Minjee and I give him encouraging nods.

"Also," Bryan adds, "I'm honestly looking forward to getting out of K-pop in the next few years. It'd be nice to be able to date someone without being afraid of breaking a contract."

I give him a sympathetic pat on the back.

"How about you, Hana?" Minjee asks me. "What's your wildest dream?"

I look first at Minjee, and then at Bryan. Part of me can't help but feel self-conscious since the two of them, with their superstar lives, will probably think my "wildest dream" is pretty ordinary. But then I remember where I'm from and what my parents do every day to help me live the life I want to live. No matter how humble my beginnings, I'm not ashamed of them.

"I want to have a long career as an actress," I say. "Whether it be in blockbuster movies or more Korean dramas. Acting is the only thing I know I'm good at, and I love it a lot, too. My parents sacrificed so much for us to just live in Korea after I got scouted. I want to make their sacrifice worth it."

"That's understandable," Minjee replies.

Bryan also nods at what I said. I guess, as teen stars, every one of us comes from families that sacrificed *something* to help us get to where we are today.

By then, we've pretty much finished eating, and we're picking at the few remaining scraps. I lean back in my chair in a content, incoming food coma state.

"How about you?" I ask Minjee, since she's the only one of us who hasn't shared anything.

She shrugs. "I honestly don't know. I got into acting and modeling pretty early. . . . My parents sort of pushed me into it as soon as I learned how to talk. Don't get me wrong, I love both things, but there's still this . . . voice in the back of my head telling me that I might only like these things because it's all I've ever known. I kind of just want to take some time off and travel a lot after I graduate from high school. Or I might take a break from the industry and go to college. We'll see."

Minjee's response surprises me, because I'd always thought that she has the perfect life, this dreamlike existence that I'd kill to have. But I guess what she said makes sense. Acting is something I *chose* for myself, while for Minjee, it's something everyone expected her to do.

"Let's hope all this *Fated Destiny* drama blows over so we can all get what we want," Bryan remarks as he gets up to throw away the now empty food containers.

Minjee and I nod grimly. This evening had been so nice

that for a brief moment, I almost forgot about all the drama. I didn't even check my phone for the entire time we had dinner.

When I first started *Fated Destiny*, I only cared about the ratings and furthering my acting career. I didn't expect to find friends in my costars, especially not friends who'd know things about me that only a handful of people do.

Somehow, regardless of everything that's going on right now, my friends make the world feel like a less scary place.

Chapter 32

EARLY NEXT MORNING, WE GET CALLED IN FOR another emergency meeting at the company headquarters. At first I think it's Mr. Kim who called the meeting, but when I enter the auditorium, I see that everyone is there *except* Mr. Kim. An elderly company representative named Mr. Kang is sitting at the front of the room, along with Director Cha and the other producers. Mr. Choi, the lead writer, is also present, as are all of our cast and crew members. I even see people I don't recognize, probably because they work in postproduction. Almost everyone in the studio conference room looks worn out, like the last several days have taken a toll on them.

I feel guilty for the trouble I've caused them, but I remind myself that I'm not the one who selfishly decided to suspend the show.

When I take a seat with my friends, everyone's eyes dart toward Minjee and me. I try to ignore the attention as best as I can.

Mr. Kang comes up to stand in the middle of the stage, the place where Mr. Kim would usually be.

Murmurs erupt from everyone present, and Mr. Kang raises his hands to motion for people to settle down.

"Thank you for gathering here today," he says, his raspy voice the complete opposite of Mr. Kim's booming one. "Some of you know who I am, but for those who don't, my name is Kang Byun-Ho and I am the CEO and founder of SBC Studios."

My jaw drops, and I'm not the only one that's shocked by the revelation. The only people that don't look surprised are the creative heads like Director Cha. I've only heard the name Kang Byun-Ho before, but never had a face to match to the name.

Mr. Kang coughs while waiting for the room to settle down again.

"I am here to announce that Mr. Kim is no longer with the company," he says. "He has been asked to step down from his position, and we are now in the process of finding someone to replace him. We at SBC were shocked by the recent revelations of the business decisions he made regarding *Fated Destiny*, and we apologize for any inconvenience they may have caused."

Minjee squeezes my hand, and I squeeze hers back. All of this sounds too good to be true.

"And after much deliberation," Mr. Kang continues, "we made the unanimous decision to resume the show."

The whole room erupts into cheers. People get up from their seats to clap, and Director Cha crosses himself while looking at the ceiling.

"We did it!" I yell, pulling both Bryan and Minjee into a group hug. We jump up and down together. It feels like Christmas all over again.

"I've been told that you are almost done with principal photography. We weren't able to premiere new episodes last week because of what happened, of course, but the viewership numbers for both broadcast and streaming reruns are stronger than ever despite the . . ." Mr. Kang trails off and gives us a pointed glance. ". . . scandal. Or perhaps *because of* it. We are still looking into exactly what caused this newfound interest in our show."

I tense up but resist the urge to comment.

This is still a win, I tell myself. *No matter what people may think of Minjee and me.*

"But yes, thank you so much for your patience as we came to this decision. Principal photography will resume tomorrow, and we will wrap within the next few weeks. We ask for your complete dedication until then. Thank you."

Everyone's happy and relieved faces fill me with so much warmth. It feels like a huge weight has been lifted off my shoulders.

But as grateful as I am that the show is quite literally going on, I remember there's still a lot more work we need to do.

"Hey," I say, turning back to my friends. "Let's go talk to Mr. Choi and Director Cha since they're both here. We need to fix the ending. More so now after everything that's happened."

"Do you think they'll really listen to us?" Minjee asks.

I shrug. "It's worth a shot. If all three of us approach them, they should at least hear us out, right?"

"True," Bryan says. "Okay, let's go."

We head down to the front row of the auditorium, where Mr. Choi and Director Cha are deep in some discussion about the logistics of the show. Mr. Choi is much smaller than the director, who looks like a giant next to the frail old man with huge glasses.

"Mr. Choi? And Director Cha?" I say, glancing at first the writer and then the director. "Could we speak with you two for a moment?"

Both Mr. Choi and Director Cha blink in surprise at us three. Director Cha looks amused, while Mr. Choi's eyebrows are creased with concern.

It's then that I realize that this is one of the only times I've ever directly interacted with Director Cha off set. Without his director's chair and the playback monitor in front of him, he looks like such a normal guy, dressed in a sweater vest and plaid shirt like he's just someone's dad.

Is Director Cha someone's dad? I wonder. I realize that I have no idea, even though I spent a good chunk of time

274

working on the show with him. Director Cha never really talks about his own personal life, and in general, sets are weird like that. You spend *months* with the same group of people to the extent that you know countless random details about their lives, but don't know about many others.

"Yes, Hana," Director Cha says. "What is it?"

I look over to Minjee and Bryan before I say the next part. They give me encouraging nods.

"We wanted to talk to you two about the ending," I say.

Mr. Choi folds his arms over his chest and mean-mugs like a bouncer at an exclusive nightclub. I swallow, losing my resolve.

"Basically, it sucks," Bryan says, cutting to the chase. Classic Bryan. "And it's really sexist. It's bad enough that the show tacked on this love triangle. But killing off both girls at the end? Come on, gentlemen, this is the twenty-first century!"

He wraps his arms around both men's shoulders, like they're all part of the same boys' club. It's the kind of flagrant deviation from Korean societal norms that only Bryan Yoon could pull off.

Looking very uncomfortable, the director and writer exchange glances.

"I really don't think the ending will fly well with anyone," I add, regaining my momentum. "Besides, this script was approved by Mr. Kim, right? Are we really going to trust his judgment? That guy hired a PI to trail us!"

Minjee nods, taking this as her cue to come in. "I talked about the ending with my parents and they were not happy with it."

"And I don't think the Brybabies will be happy with it, either!" Bryan abruptly lets go of the men. They stumble back, looking very overwhelmed. "Like, they love me and all, but they're still a very bright and socially aware group. Don't underestimate K-pop fans! Remember how involved they were in American politics?"

Both men pale at the thought. Neither of them says anything for a long moment.

"The ending is what it is because that's what Mr. Kim wanted," Director Cha finally says. "But since he's not in charge anymore . . ."

He looks to Mr. Choi, who sighs and asks, "What do you kids have in mind?"

Chapter 33

ON THE NIGHT OF THE LAST EPISODE'S PREMIERE, I invite Minjee and Bryan over to my apartment for a viewing party with my parents.

Minjee's the first to arrive, and when she comes over, Mom gives her a hug and tells her "how much prettier" she's gotten since she last came over to our place.

Minjee blushes and says, "Thank you."

We've just settled down on the couch when someone knocks on the door. Mom gets up to open it, but before she can even fully open the door, Bryan bursts in with a flourish. And he's not alone.

"Hello, everyone!" he says, dragging along a frazzled-looking boy with platinum-blond hair and round glasses. "This is Claude. Claude, meet the fam. Well, not my actual fam but you know what I mean."

Minjee and I exchange confused looks as Claude greets us in English.

"Is he the person you're dating?" I hiss at Bryan. "Or is he just a friend?"

"*Secretly* dating," Bryan says with a smirk. "I met Claude at a fashion show on one of my off days. He lives in France, but he comes with his parents to Seoul often."

"*Of course* you'd have a mysterious French boyfriend," Minjee says. "The life of Bryan Yoon is never dull."

"Shh," he says. "It's far too early for labels. After what happened with Hana and me, I've learned to take it nice and *slow*."

He waggles his eyebrows at me, and I laugh.

"I love this for you," I say. "Live your best life."

Our living room is definitely not big enough to comfortably fit six people, but tonight, everyone is in such good spirits that no one seems to mind. My parents sit on the couch while the rest of us settle onto the floor in front of the TV.

Mom hand-rolled kimbap that we can snack on while watching the show, and we're all munching on those and other Korean snacks from our neighborhood grocery store as we wait for the episode to start.

"Damn, these are some of the best kimbap I've ever had! Thank you, Umuni!" Bryan yells, politely addressing my mom by using the Korean word for "mother."

"You're welcome!" Mom says. She looks dazed, as if she still can't believe an internationally famous K-pop star like Bryan is sitting right here in our living room.

Then finally the screen goes black. Dad announces, "It's starting!"

We all hush. No one says anything throughout the opening credits. I feel a weird, bittersweet sensation when the screen says "Last Episode" after the credits. And then, we all watch as Hyun stands on top of a hill overlooking the Royal Palace.

"Looking sharp!" Minjee says, clapping Bryan on the back. He laughs, but like the rest of us, he keeps his attention glued to the screen.

"So much has changed," Hyun says in a voiceover. "Finally, there's peace, but I don't know if I can go on living like a normal high school student again."

The show then plays a sequence of flashbacks that recaps what happened throughout the entire series. Back when I was a viewer watching other K-dramas, I used to hate it when shows did this on the last episode—"They're just using old footage to fill up the air time!" I complained—but now the recap hits me differently since I can see how much I've changed throughout the show. And it's not just me. Bryan, Minjee, and even some of the supporting actors . . . we all look so much younger in the footage from the first few episodes somehow, even though we started filming this show last fall.

So much has changed. . . . I repeat Hyun's words in my thoughts. They can definitely apply to my real life, too. I take Minjee's hand and squeeze it. She squeezes back.

The episode quickly picks up after that, with Hyun

winning against the sorcerer that trapped our characters in their cycle of reincarnation. When Hyun delivers the final blow and walks off into the light, we all burst into applause for Bryan, since that's his last scene on the show.

"That was a nice finish!" I say.

He smiles like a little kid as we all pat him on the back. Claude gives Bryan a peck on the cheek, which makes me grin.

As a voiceover, Hyun goes on to talk about how he realized that the only way to truly break the cycle is to stop making the same choices he did in his previous lives.

"Sometimes," he says, "the people we think we're meant to be with aren't the ones we actually end up with, and that's okay."

The camera fades out to black and fades back in on my face.

As Sora, I look out into the distance, like Bryan was in the beginning of the episode. But instead of looking down at the palace, I'm looking at . . .

The camera slowly pans, following my gaze, the music swelling as it reaches Minjee as Danbi. We're both in our uniforms and look like normal high school students despite the fact that we just helped win a war against a powerful sorcerer. A secret smile is playing on my lips, and my eyes are shining with happiness and love. As I watch myself, I realize I wasn't acting at all in that scene. That's genuinely how I look when I'm with Minjee.

It feels bizarre, like an almost out-of-body experience. Even though I'd seen myself on-screen lots of times, I've never had a moment when I distinctly knew I wasn't really acting on camera.

Sora and Danbi walk along the beach, the same beach that I was once on with Bryan for one of the previous episodes. The joyful music continues to play, blending nicely with the ebb and flow of the waves. As Sora slips her hand into Danbi's, Sora says quietly, "It took a long time for us to finally be together, didn't it?"

"Yes," Danbi replies. "But everything leading up to this moment was worth it."

Just before the camera fades to black, Sora leans forward and gives Danbi a kiss on her forehead. It's not much, but it's enough for now.

When the closing credits start playing, everyone stands up and claps.

"And we're done!" exclaims Bryan. "Yay, us!"

Minjee, Bryan, and I get into a group hug. My parents take pictures to capture the moment.

"Congratulations!" Mom says.

She hugs me while Dad gives Bryan a pat on the back, just before Claude wraps him into a tight hug. Both Bryan and Claude get this intense look in their eyes, and I'm almost afraid they're going to make out right in front of my parents when they burst into nervous laughter.

"I am so proud of you," Mom tells me. "Your first show as a lead actress."

"Yes," Dad agrees. "It was a great finish. Congrats to all of you."

Almost immediately, our phones start buzzing with notifications. I check social media and see that we're trending #1 in the Korean entertainment news.

Fated Destiny Delivers Unexpected Twist in Final Episode

Fated to Be Without a Prince? Recapping the
Last Episode of *Fated Destiny*

What Happened to Bryan? A Discussion on How a
Show's Top Star Didn't End Up with Either of the Girls,
and How This May Be the Better, Braver Choice

Aside from the news, the audience's reactions are pure chaos. People are either screaming about "history being made" or bemoaning what they see as a sign of the end of the world.

Bryan laughs at some of the reactions. "Well, it looks like we did it. Everyone's rocked to the core about the ending."

"Hey, buzz is buzz," I say, repeating the words Sophia told me a long time ago. "Good or bad, the studio will get the viewership numbers they want."

In the end, that argument is how I convinced the higher-ups to get on board with the idea in the first place. I still can't believe we managed to pull it off. While I was growing up, I only saw Korean dramas and movies where queer people suffered or even sometimes died a tragic death. But that didn't happen today. And I can hardly believe that I was part of this positive change.

"We really did it," says Minjee, echoing my thoughts. From her awed expression, I can tell she's thinking the same things as I was. "So many kudos for coming up with the idea, Hana."

Everyone claps for me.

"Thanks," I reply when it quiets down. "But none of this would have been possible without you."

Minjee and I look into each other's eyes. Now *Minjee and I* are the ones that are about to make out right in front of my parents.

Bryan loudly coughs.

"And you, Bryan," I add, low-key grateful for the interruption. "And you."

Everyone laughs. I pull my friends into a hug.

"No, but seriously. Thanks. Both of you. Without you guys backing me up, we probably wouldn't have been able to convince everyone to change the script."

"No problem," Bryan says.

Minjee gives me a thumbs-up.

"All right, who's up for some celebrating?"

I turn around to see Mom holding up an ice cream cake with a handful of candles on top. The cake looks like it should belong in a freakin' art museum. I marvel at the intricate fruit overlays and icing designs, which again look too beautiful to eat.

"Mom!" I exclaim. "Wow, how did I not notice this cake

was in the freezer this entire time?"

"I have my ways," Mom says with a wink.

"She hid them behind the bags of steamed buns and dumplings," explains Dad, causing everyone to laugh. "One of these days, when you guys are all of age, we can all do a toast. Until then . . ."

He gets up and takes out cans of Chilsung Cider from the fridge.

"Soda and ice cream cake!" Minjee exclaims. "I feel like I'm five again."

"Forgive me, but . . ." Claude says in French-accented English, peering curiously at the white-and-green cans. "I've never had this . . . cider. What is it?"

"It's kind of like Sprite but better," I explain in English. "In my opinion, anyway. Try it!"

Dad hands Claude a can, and he pops one open and takes a sip.

"C'est magnifique!" Claude exclaims, making us all laugh.

My parents place the cake and the rest of the soda on the coffee table, and we all sit back down on the living room floor. As we're eating and drinking, my parents ask Claude about France, while Bryan, Minjee, and I talk about how we should all go on a trip together to celebrate the end of *Fated Destiny*.

"What about Australia?" Bryan suggests. "I've always wanted to go see the kangaroos."

"*Australia?*" Minjee asks. "That's so random."

"School's going to start soon, so we probably can't go

anywhere far," I point out. "I still have some reading to catch up on, too."

"Oh, that's right," Bryan says. "You and Minjee are taking in-person classes this year. I guess I'll just go with Claude."

He nudges Claude, who shifts his focus to us. "Go where?"

"Australia!" Bryan claps him on the back. "We're going to go see kangaroos and koalas!"

"Ooh, I've always wanted to go!" Claude replies instantly. "When are we going? Next week?"

Minjee and I burst out laughing. I'm cackling so much that it gets hard to breathe.

"Bryan," I say between gasps for air. "You and Claude are meant to be."

Bryan waggles his eyebrows. "I guess you could say it's . . . *fated destiny.*"

Everyone's laughing now, and we toast our cans of cider.

"To Bryan and Claude!" Minjee exclaims. "And to us being done with *Fated Destiny*!"

We all cheer.

The last few months have been so wild, and I can barely believe everything that's happened. Not even in my dreams could I have imagined that I would ever be sitting in the middle of my family's Seoul apartment with my girlfriend on one side and my fake ex-boyfriend on the other.

I take another sip of my cider and eat my last sugary piece of ice cream cake.

"Hey," Minjee says.

"Hm?"

When I turn toward her, she smears cake on my cheek.

We burst into giggles.

Bryan's first to notice what's going on. And then Mom. Soon, everyone's cracking up again. Dad lovingly smears cake on Mom's face, which makes us laugh even harder.

The left side of my face still covered with cake, I wrap my arms around Minjee and hug her tight.

Epilogue

FIVE MONTHS LATER

FATED DESTINY ENDS UP BEING LABELED "THE most controversial show of the year" and ranked at the top of the ratings of its season. Not all the attention is good—Minjee and I had to put our social medias on private to avoid some of the hate we got—but I do receive offers to audition for more movies and TV shows, which is more than I thought I'd be getting from this fallout.

In the end, though, Minjee and I both decide to take a break from the entertainment industry to focus on school. I love acting, but after all the craziness and drama related to *Fated Destiny*, I missed the relative peace of being a student.

"Now that the semester's over, do you want to slowly ease back into the industry?" Sophia asks me on the phone. "I know Korean summer vacations aren't super long, but maybe you can take some time to audition! You got some pretty amazing offers. Even ones from Hollywood!"

"Dang, you go, girl!" Minjee says, patting me on the shoulder.

I have Sophia on speaker, since Minjee and I are in her family's car, driving to the beach where we shot the last scene of *Fated Destiny*. Neither of us had ever seen what the beach looked like in the summer before, so we decided to go on a road trip to get away from everything in the city.

I hesitate before giving Sophia a response. "I'll think on it," I say. "Can I give you my answer some other time? I want to enjoy my summer first."

"Yes, most definitely!" Sophia says. "Enjoy being a kid. But also keep in mind that this buzz from *Fated Destiny* won't last long."

"Okay," I reply. "Thanks, Sophia."

I let out a deep sigh after we hang up.

"Hana!" Minjee cries out in frustration. "How long are you going to take a break from the industry? *Hollywood* wants you! You should at least audition."

"I know, I know," I reply. "But our lives pretty much blew up because of the show. I don't really want to experience that again anytime soon."

Minjee's expression softens. "Okay, fair."

Even though everything ultimately worked out, things were very stressful for a while. Outside of all the chaos of social media and the news, I was lucky that my parents accepted me when I came out right away. But Minjee's parents didn't talk to her for a whole month, avoiding her whenever they could. For the longest time, we were afraid that she was going to get kicked out and were actually surprised when Minjee's parents—albeit begrudgingly—accepted her sexuality in the end.

"What if me being in the spotlight again brings more attention to us? To you?" I ask softly, placing a hand on her cheek. Minjee looks down at my hand, her expression unreadable.

"Miss?" says the driver then. "We're here."

"Thank you." Minjee pulls away from me to get out of the car.

I follow suit, getting out on my side.

We don't say anything to each other for a while as we walk along the beach. Everything else around us is totally different from the way it was when we shot scenes here several months ago. Instead of being gray and stormy, the sky is bright blue with not a cloud in sight. The sand, which looked so pale before, is golden with warm sunlight. And probably the most striking is the number of people crowded along the beach, a stark contrast from how deserted this place was before.

Minjee stops so abruptly that I almost run into her.

"You shouldn't let your fear of what might happen to us prevent you from pursuing your dreams," she blurts out. "I took a hiatus from the industry because I *wanted* to. It's something I've been meaning to do for a long time. I never loved acting like you do, and I want to find something else that *I'm* passionate about. Don't worry about me."

"I know that." I sigh, looking down at the sand. "I appreciate you telling me that, though. I'm just . . . scared, I guess. What happened with our show was amazing, but then people started scrutinizing our every move. It made me wonder if everything we did was worth it."

"It was," Minjee says, sounding absentminded. "Hana, look."

She points at the coastline, where we filmed the final scene of *Fated Destiny*. There are so many people along the beach, so at first I have no idea what she wants me to look at.

But then I spot them.

Two girls walk side by side, dressed in school uniforms, just like how Minjee and I were when we shot our scene. They look like they're in middle school, maybe a few years younger than us. Even though they're holding hands, at first glance, they look like they're just friends. But as I watch, the taller one leans down and kisses the other girl on the forehead, just like how I kissed Minjee in the last episode of *Fated Destiny*.

My heart feels like it's grown five sizes. I'm filled with so much warmth and happiness that I can't even say a single word.

"So, the real reason why I wanted to bring you here," Minjee says with a sly grin, "is because I heard that ever since our show ended, this beach became a prime location for fans of the show. Namely the *queer* fans. Apparently, this was formerly a key location for *Goblin* and other K-dramas and even a BTS music video at one point. But now queer teens are claiming this beach as their own."

"We did that?" I say when I'm finally able to speak. Tears prickle at the corners of my eyes as I spot yet another pair of girls walking side by side together.

"Yup," Minjee replies. "Well, *you* did. Because it was *your* idea."

"To be fair, it started off as a joke." I laugh, my voice sounding weird and garbled since I'm trying so hard not to start bawling.

Minjee laughs. "As many ingenious ideas do. But don't you see? We *need* more queer content on TV, especially in K-dramas. And we need queer actresses like you to help people feel seen. This may be selfish of me, but *I'm* certainly not going to be one of them. The more I spend time away from it, the more I realize acting really isn't for me. But you, Hana? You live and *breathe* acting. I can see it every time we're together on set. You should see the way your eyes light up when you're in character! Please don't give this up."

I laugh and pull Minjee into a hug. "I love you," I say. "Thank you for everything."

"I love you, too."

She nestles her head against my shoulder. We stay there like that for a long moment, staring out into the turquoise waters.

And then, when I'm ready, I call Sophia back.

Acknowledgments

I probably say this with every book I write, but this project was the hardest one I've worked on in a while. Not only is writing the infamous "Book Two" challenging, but COVID-19—like it did for everyone—shook up everything from when this book was supposed to be published to my personal life. Because of all of this, I am all the more grateful to everyone who made this book possible.

First and foremost, I would like to thank Mabel Hsu, my editor, for her ingenious editing prowess and dedication. COVID-19 hit the publishing industry and professionals alike hard, and I can't even begin to imagine the long hours she and the other members of my team pulled to make things happen. From the many emails to the off-hours video chat with me while I was in South Korea as part of my research trip for this book, Mabel really did the most for me and this project. Thank you so much to Mabel and the rest of my team at HarperCollins.

Second, I would like to thank my agent, Penny Moore, who is as always my number one cheerleader and advocate for my books. Publishing is almost never a smooth ride, and I always feel so lucky to have her to help me navigate the waters. Sophia is only a badass because Penny is.

Working two jobs—especially during a pandemic—is never easy, and I count myself very lucky to *somehow* get by every week. In 2021, I honestly couldn't have juggled all that I do without my partner, Sean Dilliard. Thank you for making sure I still eat meals, drink enough water, and get a reasonable amount of sleep. Your love and support truly get me through my hardest days.

I would not have been able to write this book without my entire childhood (and adulthood!) of watching K-dramas. In particular, some shows that inspired and informed this book are *The Greatest Love* (2011), *Queen In-hyun's Man* (2012), *Guardian: The Lonely and Great God - Goblin* (2016), *Man to Man* (2017), *Mystic Pop-Up Bar* (2020), and *Itaewon Class* (2020). Thank you to all the talent and creatives involved in making these shows.

Equally important to the book are the many years I spent traveling around South Korea, both when I actually lived in the country and did not. I couldn't have done any of that exploring without my family and friends, who took me around almost all the places mentioned in this book. A special thanks goes to my mom, for taking me around Seoul in the middle of a pandemic (masks on, of course) as I was struggling to write various scenes in this book (and for the many hours we spent watching K-dramas together throughout my childhood!). Thank you also to Sharon Choi, who introduced me to Ikseon-dong, and for just in general being an awesome friend and human being.

I also couldn't have written a book about a TV show without the years I spent on set and in class during my time at the University of Southern California School of Cinematic Arts or on the Universal Studios lot. Obviously, the world of K-dramas is *way* different from Hollywood, but I'd still like to thank all the professors, mentors, and friends I met in Los Angeles for instilling in me a deep love of movies and TV shows of all forms.

On an unrelated note, I want to thank my other friends, without whom I would not have been able to get through the last few years. Thank you to Brianna Lei, Francesca Flores, Aneeqah Naeem, Alice Zhu, Bernice Yau, Shiyun Sun, Luke Chou, Chelsea Chang, Annie Lee, Kaiti Liu, Angelica Tran, Stephanie Lu, Rey Noble, Anita Chen, Amelie Wen Zhao, Mason Deaver, Sarah Wu, Axie Oh, and many others that my sleep-deprived brain is probably blanking on right now. A million thank-yous would not be enough.

Finally, I would like to thank all the readers, booksellers, librarians, teachers, and parents who've supported my books. Most of the Mindy Kim books and my YA debut, *I'll Be the*

One, came out during the pandemic. Naturally, things have been very rough. Even so, I am grateful for every social media post, review, video, fan art, lesson plan, etc. that you've made for my books. I feel honored whenever someone says they love my writing. Thank you so much for your support in these trying times.